The Divinity Laws

PJ King

With my sincerest thanks to:

A.M. - for editing this book; putting up with my Yoda-tendencies; and the many amusing post-it notes that accompanied your notes.

My family – for continuing to love and support me, as you always have. I don't know where I would be without you.

My Creator – the author and finisher of my faith...
(Hebrews 12: 2)

Visit the author's website at
www.pjkingblog.wordpress.com

First Edition.

ISBN: 9781521138427

Contents

Prologue

There had been another report of the underground movement. There were definitely more reports these days. This one coincided with a blackwashing just a couple of days ago. It was unusual to get more than two reports in a month, but this latest one was the seventh in just three weeks. The month before they'd had five: three blackwashings, one underground movement and an accusation that turned out to be a hoax.

The blackwashings didn't bother Marson so much. There had always been blackwashings. Ninety-nine per cent of the time they were easy to process and in most of those instances, they were simple cases of deviancy fuelled by other issues: financial problems, mental breakdowns, teenage high spirits; on one occasion a bump on the head had triggered the deviancy, and in at least ten per cent of the cases, the individual already had criminal convictions. There had always been fluctuations in the levels of blackwashing too; these seemed to be influenced by social and cultural factors. There was always a rise around the old festival times for example, especially Crissmass when the long winter was making people feel especially lonely and low.

The latest blackwashing appeared to be an isolated case in the countryside: one of the villages on the edge of the suburban sprawl (one more housing development and it would *be* the suburban sprawl) where a teacher had been blackwashed by a pupil. Marson scrolled through the report file: male, history teacher, living in the village, working at the school for six months, single, with family in the north of the country, mid-forties, probably having a midlife crisis.

Marson closed the file and flagged it as important. The local police would be dealing with the case but it was best to keep half an eye on it; you just never knew if it might turn out to be more than it appeared. It wasn't that the police were incapable of dealing with these situations, but they didn't always treat them as seriously as they should. They did not have the specialised knowledge of the Division and there was a tendency to treat the perpetrators as merely time-wasting lunatics. The fact was, although the individuals might not have pulled a bank job or murdered their neighbour, they had still broken the law, and that made them criminals. The Division preferred to use the term 'deviants' (or 'deves' as the younger generation had dubbed it) because it suggested an opportunity for correction and rehabilitation which, after all, was the primary aim of its work. Because of this, it was easy for the police to be flippant about such cases. Marson didn't like to, but on occasions it had been necessary to intervene in an investigation. This was always met with hostility; nobody liked having to hand over to the Divinity Division. Marson was aware of the irony in the name. As firemen put out fires, Divinity Agents dealt with the potentially incendiary cases of deviants who broke the Divinity Laws.

Even the police would admit that the Divinity Laws were now the foundation of every civilised society. Virtually every country across the world had adopted some version of the laws in order to maintain peace and order. That's why the work of the Divinity Division was so important. It only took one undetected deviant to create several others. It didn't take long for several deviants to become twenty, and twenty to grow into a hundred and then the hundred to spread across the rest of the country, turning ordinary citizens into deviants wherever they went. That's why it was the underground movement reports which concerned Marson the most.

Marson found the new report and stared sternly at the information on the screen. A frown worked on deepening the furrow in his brow. This report came from a city area, as they often did: another suspected gathering of the underground group known as The Assembly. So there had to be at least one undetected deviant operating under their noses. These were notoriously difficult to trace. A lone deviant was particularly vulnerable and likely to be 'blackwashed': exposed as a breaker of the Divinity Laws and their deviancy reported to the Division. Blackwashing, for a lone deviant, was inevitable. But a pair of deviants, was less likely to be discovered. That was why it was best to keep an eye on the individual blackwashings: just in case, by a slim chance, a second deviant had stayed under the radar.

Chapter One

The halfpipe looked like the unfinished hull of a ship, beached on the edge of a tarmac island. It stood apart from the rest of the playground, guarding the rail that divided the tarmac from a sea of grass which spread out to cracked paths caging it in on three sides. In the whole of the recreation ground, the top of the halfpipe was the best place to get a view of the harbour below the village. From ground level all that was visible of the bay was a smudge of blue between trees and roof tops, but on top of the concrete shell, on this clear burning summer's day, the harbour waters glistened as an expanse of sapphire blue set with the emeralds of small islands, with the glint of white sails passing by.

Clara hadn't realised this view existed until she had gripped the hot rungs of the ladder and climbed to the top of the halfpipe platform. She had looked down at first, where the concrete plunged down from her feet into a long bowl before rising again to complete the symmetry. The heat radiated up from the surface and hit her bare legs as she stood nervously on the edge. The bottom of the pipe looked flat and hard. Her skin tingled instinctively, imagining the impact of the concrete on her naked flesh. She looked at the board under her foot, unfamiliar and treacherous. They wanted her to ride it down one wall of the halfpipe and up the other. They wanted her to fail - the boys, the Boarders. They wanted to watch her fall; they were expecting it. It was inevitable: the impact with the concrete, the pain and raw skin, the humiliation.

Her stomach tightened and then she looked to her left. What a view. She hadn't known this existed. She wondered if the Boarders saw it when they came up here, or was it so common to them that they no longer looked? She could look at it forever. Her stomach muscles relaxed and she breathed in gently the calm sea air.

"Ready?" a voice sneered, interrupting her forgetfulness.

Clara looked back down at the skateboard and the concrete below her. There would be pain; but it would be temporary. And with that certainty, she pushed off from the edge.

The rough roll of wheels rumbled through her, the board wobbled dangerously, she cleared the expanse of the bowl and felt the change in gradient as it curved into the opposite wall. This was where she and the board parted ways, the latter abandoning the journey and clattering down into the base of the pipe. She followed it seconds later, scraping a knee down the face of the wall and leaving the skin from her hands on the hot concrete. She managed to twist on to her back as she hit the bottom of the pipe and end up in a sitting position, legs straight out in front of her.

"Clara!" Jena yelled, leaping up next to her, "Are you all right?"

Clara nodded mutely, staring ahead of her: another new view. She hadn't seen this one before either. She heard Jena give a snort of disgust as she followed her gaze.

"Pathetic. Come on."

But Clara couldn't drag her eyes away yet. The letters loomed over her from the curve in the wall as if ready to leap on her: D.E.V.E.

"Come on, Clara," Jena insisted, pulling at her arm.

Clara looked down at her legs where a trickle of red oozed from one knee, and then down at her lap where she was cradling her right wrist. Only now did she hear the smirks.

"C'mon ladies. Don't take all day."

Clara allowed Jena to drag her off the halfpipe, and then the pain bubbled up in place of adrenaline.

"You know what we'll do if you come back," one of the boys said calmly, shaking a spray can of paint at them. Jena manoeuvred her past them with a snarl. Clara tried to resist looking back, but couldn't help a last glance over her shoulder at the concrete hull. She felt a wistful pang in her gut for the view and then for the roll of wheels and the rush through her veins.

*

"You did what?" Carver asked with his usual dry incredulity.

"Fell off a skateboard," Clara replied.

"You got her into trouble, didn't you?" Carver said over her head at Jena.

"I did not!" Jena protested.

Clara kept dabbing her knee with spit and tissue as if the conversation had nothing to do with her. This was typical Carver and Jena.

"You stuck your nose into their business," Carver continued, "Don't you know what Boarders are like?"

"They were graffitiing the halfpipe."

"It's their halfpipe."

Jena snorted with disgust. "That's what 'Ash' said. It's public property and graffitiing public property is illegal."

"So how come Clara ends up in the middle of it?"

"Listen, you idiot..."

It was time to interrupt. "I agreed," Clara said simply, giving up on her knee and kicking her heels against the brick wall.

"To ride a skateboard on the halfpipe?"

"You know me," she smiled and rolled her eyes, "Can't resist a challenge – total adrenalin junkie. Anything to get a high."

Carver gave one of his short, dry laughs and Jena snorted again, this time with cynicism.

"You enjoyed it didn't you?" Carver said with a keen sideways look.

"Of course she didn't enjoy it," Jena cut in, "She fell off. No one enjoys falling."

"Yeah?" Carver challenged, "Bungee jumpers, skydivers, tombstoners..."

"Bungee rope, parachutes...," Jena shot back, "No one plans to fall and kill themselves."

"But there's always the possibility. That's what gives you the thrill – hoping you won't fall and kill yourself, hoping the 'chute opens – the anticipation of danger."

"Rubbish."

Trying to stop Jena and Carver from fighting was like trying to stop a cat from going after a mouse. It required distracting the cat and hoping the mouse would have the sense to run for cover. Clara wasn't always sure who was the cat and who was the mouse but, as the one always stuck in the middle, she was always in need of a distraction.

"Do you think Boarders mean it when they threaten you?" she asked.

"Ugh!" Jena responded, "Come back again darlin'," she said in a dumb-sounding voice, "And we'll give youse a real makeover. Huhhuhhuh."

Carver raised an eyebrow. "Yes," he said, "They do." He slid off the wall, "Maybe you should learn," he said to Clara, with a mischievous smile.

"Learn what?"

"To skateboard - since you enjoyed it so much…"

"Don't you dare!" Jena exclaimed to Clara, "I'd never speak to you again."

"Sounds like the perfect reason…"

"Shove off, Carver," Jena hissed.

Carver shrugged and stuck out his tongue before sauntering back to the house next door.

"Freak," Jena muttered after him.

"Don't," Clara said quietly, "He's all right."

"I don't know how you can stand him living next door - always just over the fence." Jena glanced over her shoulder and slid off the wall. "I should go," she said with a nod at the house behind them.

Clara followed her gaze to catch a twitch of the curtain at the front window.

"I have to pack," Jena added.

"Ah. The tropical holiday."

"Yes, do think of me," Jena smiled, tossing back her dark hair dramatically and slipping on her sunglasses, "When I'm sitting on a golden beach, being served a mocktail by a handsome waiter…"

Clara made a face of mock disgust. "You'd better bring me back something."

"Hey, I'm sorry by the way…" Jena wrapped her arms suddenly round Clara's shoulders, "For getting you into trouble. Thanks for bailing me out, you're a real friend."

Clara swallowed awkwardly and patted Jena's arms in surprise.

Jena released her with a perfect grin on her face. "Catch you tomorrow," she sang aloud, strolling with a confident bounce up the road.

Clara watched her until she turned the corner and then looked over her shoulder again at her own house. With a thoughtful pursing of her mouth, she swivelled on the wall, dropped onto the small square of lawn and limped to the front door.

The hall was cool and dark compared with the heat and glare of the street. Clara gingerly dusted herself off and smoothed her hair with one hand, before following the 'clack, clack' of a knife into the kitchen.

Sandy was standing at one counter dicing vegetables rhythmically, her back tall and straight, hair swept up into a neat swirl, one shoulder barely moving with the expert movement of the blade in her hand. The clacking stopped and, taking a sidestep to the right, she slid the contents of the board into the pan of hot oil on the stove. The oil spat and hissed. Sandy half turned to look at Clara, giving her an appraising look up and down before she reached for a wooden spoon and started stirring the contents of the sizzling pan.

"Been out with Jena?" she asked.

"Yes," Clara answered, crossing to the sink to wash her hands, "At the park."

"What have you done to yourself?"

"I fell off a skateboard."

Her aunt gave a small sigh of irritation. "Really?"

Clara gave her perfectly-vertical back a curious look.

"I received an email from your parents," Sandy continued, "They are supposed to come home next week, but they've had to extend their stay for a fortnight beyond that; so they won't be back for another three weeks now. They wanted to know if your uncle and I would continue our visit here for that time."

"Oh...," Clara responded vaguely,

tenderly drying her hands.

"I agreed. Apparently there's a letter in the post for you."

Clara took an apple from the fruit bowl and carefully lifted the garage keys from the hook, watching her aunt's back while she had placed another vegetable on the chopping board. The 'clack, clack' of the knife began again.

"I don't know why they don't just email you. It would get to you a lot quicker."

Clara slipped the keys into her pocket. "It's just something more tangible," she said.

Her aunt let out a sharp breath through her nostrils that, in anyone less ladylike, would be interpreted as a snort. "I'm out for dinner," she said, "I'll leave this in the fridge and you can reheat it when your uncle gets in."

"Thank you." Clara bit into her apple, hesitated at the kitchen door for a moment and when no further conversation was forthcoming, slipped out to the garden.

Clara jumped a little as a spider scuttled away from the light which flooded the garage floor and disappeared under the workbench. The smell of damp filled her nostrils as she edged warily into the crowded space, one eye searching for anything else of the eight legged kind. The garage was like almost any other garage on the street, housing all sorts of items except a car. Clara had to move half a bike and a standard lamp before she could squeeze between the chest freezer and the lawnmower to get at what she wanted. Greg's boxes were clearly identifiable with his name scrawled in fat black letters on every side. They were sealed with packing tape which Clara slit open with a pair of secateurs. The first box had a lot of paperwork in it, so was surprisingly heavy to move when she tried to get to the box underneath it. The next contained old films and music albums, a pair of speakers and a defunct hard drive, but the third had just what she was looking for, right at the top. Clara took out the skateboard and carefully dusted it down on her shorts. It looked old and tatty, but it was in one piece and the wheels made a satisfying 'whirr, whirr' when she span them.

She carefully re-stacked Greg's boxes before squeezing back out into the sunlight. She locked the garage and then stood swinging the keys on one finger whilst she considered whether it was possible to get the skateboard into the house without being seen by Sandy. It was worth trying, if her aunt was still cooking in the kitchen. Or she could put the skateboard back where she had found it. What did she need it for? Carver's suggestion was only a joke. She should unlock the garage and put it back. But even as she agreed with this idea, she carried the board into the house with her.

Once in her room, Clara slid the board under her bed and grabbed a book from her bedside table. Slipping off her shoes, she curled up on the window seat and rested the book on her lap. She lifted a section of the windowsill and took out a folded piece of paper from the small cavity underneath. Carefully unfolding the paper, she laid it across the opened book and drew her knees up. A shallow pool of blood had collected in the jagged edges of the torn skin on her right knee. She would have to put a plaster on it later. Carefully, she smoothed the paper, but she didn't read it straight away. Her mind drifted off to the view of the harbour from the top of the halfpipe and the rumble of wheels through her bones and then the graffitied word on the halfpipe wall: DEVE.

A crude, almost obscene word, designed to offend in a meaningless sort of way – mere decoration in this context. Yet to apply it directly to a person was quite another matter. A serious matter. It was an accusation then: the sort that could get the recipient in all sorts of trouble. Only Boarders would have the audacity to spray the term on their property – it was the same audacity that allowed them to 'ban' others from the park, as if they owned it. Jena was right; it wasn't their property. And Carver was right too; Boarders didn't make empty threats. So a person would have to be careful if using the park without them knowing.

There must be times when the Boarders would leave. The park would be empty. The halfpipe deserted. But if she was caught…

Clara looked at the paper spread on the open pages of the book in front of her. There were worse things to be caught at…

She stared pensively out of the window again and it was a good five minutes before she noticed Carver pulling faces at her from the opposite window. Clara made a face back and then pulled down the blind, shutting him and the perilous world out.

*

"A school teacher has today been arrested on deviancy charges. Hatherhay Summers, who taught at Greylinghurst Secondary School, was reported to police by a pupil after allegedly breaking the Law of Witness. Further investigation is underway and the trial will take place…"

Carver switched the broadcast to mute and poked a fork at his dinner thoughtfully.

So, Mr Summers was a deviant. It just went to show you could never tell. He wondered how long he had been keeping that secret and who had blackwashed him. It always happened in the end; they were always blackwashed. Secrets had a way of coming to light, especially with deviants. It was as if they couldn't help themselves. You'd think keeping your own secret would be easy, especially if it was something as simple as a belief or idea, but something always brought it out in the end. It was their own fault really.

Still, Carver felt sorry for Mr Summers. The trial would be merely a formality to determine the nature and extent of his deviancy. He would be found guilty, sentenced to a rehabilitation centre and, when he got out, he would never teach again. He would probably have to move where no one knew him, take up a new career, start afresh.

Carver suddenly wasn't hungry anymore. He got up from the kitchen stool and pushed the remains of his meal off the plate and into the bin.

It was a shame. Mr Summers had been a good history teacher and he had always looked forward to his lessons. But you never could tell with people. Unless you knew them well enough you'd never see the signs, and even then you might still miss it until it was too late. Until they were too far gone. Until they had broken the Divinity Laws. Once that happened, there was no going back.

Chapter Two

The morning was enticing enough to lure her aunt and uncle out earlier than usual. At ten o'clock, they drove up the road in their sports car with a picnic basket and the instruction that Clara was not to go anywhere on her own.

Clara was closing the front door behind her at five past ten, skateboard in one hand. She hesitated for a moment at the garden gate, holding the board gingerly as if it was a neon sign that read 'Stolen Property'. She knew if she met any of her peers she would be looked at strangely for having such an item on her. Clearly, a fifteen-year-old girl from the village suburbs and a shabby board didn't belong together. It's Greg's board, Clara told herself repeatedly, and I'm just lending it to a friend. I have no intention of using it myself. Perhaps if she believed it, that's what it would look like.

As it was, she didn't meet anyone else on her way to the recreation ground. The park was full of Boarders and no one else. None of them were skating. In fact, they all seemed to be congregated in the middle of the halfpipe, looking at something on one wall.

Clara skirted round to the West wall of the park where it was high enough for her to lean on and far enough away for her to observe the halfpipe without being noticed. There was a lot of gesturing going on amongst the angry tones of conversation. She recognised Ash from the day before, in the middle of the group, giving some sort of instruction.

"I knew you'd come back," a familiar voice at her shoulder said with a sneer.

Clara glanced sideways at Carver as he mimicked her stance and leant with his arms crossed on the wall. "You enjoy sneaking up on people?"

"You enjoy spying on Boarders?"

She didn't reply but gave him a wry smile.

"I hope you're not thinking of going into the park," Carver continued lightly, "You know what they said they'd do if they caught you here again."

"So I won't get caught."

Carver snorted. "I knew you enjoyed it," he said gleefully, "You want to do it again, don't you? Is that Greg's board?"

"Yes." She rested her chin on her arms and gave him a thoughtful look.

Carver returned it with a shrug. "Don't get caught," he said seriously, and then grinned and reverted to his usual mocking tone, "Especially by Jena." He straightened and vaulted easily over the wall into the park.

Clara watched him cross towards the halfpipe, pass it on the near side and step over the rail on to the field.

In the crowd of Boarders, Ash dropped off the pipe and gave a signal to the group. Almost immediately, they followed him as he left the park and headed down the high street. In a moment, the gate clanged shut behind the last of them and the park was empty. Clara picked up the board and dropped it over the wall before climbing over. Retrieving the board and holding it close against one leg, as if she could hide it from view, she crossed the tarmac cautiously to the hull of the halfpipe. Her heart beat quickly and the middle finger of her left hand tapped rhythmically against the thumb. She was nervous, not just because Carver was right: if she got caught she would be in trouble. The Boarders had given a clear warning yesterday about not coming back to 'their park'. She had Jena to thank for that, but that wasn't what she was afraid of. If the Boarders caught her on their halfpipe with her borrowed, tatty skateboard, they would laugh her to death; then she really would never be able to show her face here again.

The halfpipe looked just as imposing as it had done the day before and just as unforgiving. Clara winced inwardly at the memory of hitting the hot surface and felt her muscles tighten in response. Her common sense told her this wasn't a good idea, but her curiosity encouraged her forward, like the suggestive voice that urges you to get a little closer to the edge of a cliff for a better view. It's just looking, it told her. Just get a feel for it, that's all you have to do. It's perfectly safe.

Climbing into the bowl of the pipe was like stepping into the toothless mouth of a yawning creature. If she disturbed it with her clumsiness, it might swallow her for being so foolish. It felt different today, emptier and bigger. Clara put down the board and stared at the wall she had stared at yesterday, when she'd been sprawled on the floor of the pipe. DEVE still leapt out from the wall, but then her eyes were drawn to where, in letters of equal size and boldness, the word IVINE dropped down from the D.

DIVINE.

This was even worse than DEVE. DIVINE was not only offensive, it was illegal. Anyone who saw this would take it as a public declaration – a breaking of the Laws. Left long enough, it would draw the attention of the Divinity Division. Clara felt her stomach tighten at the thought, but another sensation also rose at the same time in her chest. Who would write this? It was too dangerous to be a joke. Only someone who wanted to create trouble would paint this. Or a deviant – one prepared to risk exposure. Only a lone deviant would be that desperate. This was a bad sign and Clara's impulse told her to leave immediately - though a conflicting fascination compelled her to stay.

Clara was still staring at the wall when a voice addressed her from the tarmac: "You shouldn't be here."

She dragged her gaze away from the wall to where the speaker stood next to the halfpipe, looking up at her. He was a typical Boarder, in a red hoody, frayed jeans and trainers. His fair hair was tousled as if he'd just got out of bed and he wore the black leather strap on his wrist that all Boarders wore as some sort of identity tag. He put his hands in his pockets and eyed her critically with intelligent blue eyes.

"Who did that?" Clara asked, indicating the new graffiti.

He shrugged, "Not us." He stepped up next to her, "You don't take threats seriously then?" He was considering her in much the same way a cat considers a stray mouse after it's just eaten its fill of them; the natural instinct was there, but there was doubt over whether the chase was entirely necessary.

Clara took in the calm gaze which he fixed on her, his height and the natural casualness of his movements. She would bet he was fast when he needed to be.

"So who did it?"

"Don't know," he shrugged, "It appeared overnight. Someone's idea of a sick joke, I guess. Your friend wouldn't approve."

Clara smiled. He seemed to make up his mind about her and indicated her board with a nod.

"Yours?"

"Yes."

He flicked one end with his foot and the board flipped upwards so the other end met his fingertips. He lifted it briefly and glanced over it. "Old board."

"It was my brother's."

He raised an eyebrow. "Your brother was a Boarder?"

"Not exactly."

He dropped the board and stood back to look at her. "You want to skate?" It was more of a statement than a question. "I'll teach you."

"Why?"

"Tenner a week." It was an honest answer. "Meet me here at ten thirty a.m. any day you like and I'll teach you to skate."

Clara gave him a long, careful look. A tenner a week was most of her holiday fund. What if she paid him and he never turned up? On top of that, it was a crazy idea anyway.

"Deal." she agreed.

"Good," he said and flipped the board up again into his hand, "Learn to do that first. It'll save you a lot of back ache."

She took the board from him.

"And don't come into the park again on your own." he added matter-of-factly, "They will do what they said, and I won't stop them. This is a business deal only."

Clara believed him. She hesitated for a moment. "What's your name?"

"Flinn."

"I'm...," she began, automatically holding out a hand, and then feeling socially backwards.

"Clara. I remember."

She smiled shyly, shoving her hand into her pocket as the memory of the whole incident came flooding back. She glanced back at the graffitied wall and then leapt off the halfpipe and stepped over the rail on to the grass. Flinn was watching her as she looked back briefly over her shoulder, as if he might change his mind about letting her off so easily. She smiled as she turned away and started across the field, carrying the board a little more confidently than before. She was halfway across the grass when she saw Carver coming in the opposite direction.

"I forgot to mention," he said, handing her

an envelope, "You have a letter."

"You intercepted my post?"

"It's from your parents, I'm guessing."

Clara felt something lift inside. She had been waiting for this for weeks. Something tangible at last, paper they had touched covered in foreign dust, pages scrawled over with familiar handwriting. Her parents didn't have frequent access to a phone or internet, so this was the next best thing; when she read it, she would hear their voices in her head.

"Thanks, Carver," she said gently.

"Uh oh. Incoming," Carver said suddenly. He grabbed the board from her and Clara turned to see Jena crossing the grass towards them.

Wearing an oversized hat, sunglasses and a floral-print dress that floated about her legs as she walked, Jena looked as if she had just stepped off a sun-soaked beach. The only thing that gave her away was her pearl-white skin. She skipped the last few feet and flung her arms around Clara's neck, knocking her hat from her head.

"We're off in an hour! Thought I'd say a last goodbye!" she laughed and swooped down to scoop up her hat from the brittle grass. Her eyes narrowed as she noticed Carver with the skateboard in his hand. "I don't think you're the Boarder type, Carver," she sneered.

"Enjoy your holiday, Jena," Carver said sweetly, "Don't hurry back - or ever, for that matter."

"Well, I hope it rains here - the entire two weeks," Jena scowled back. "Sorry Clara, of course I don't, but... what is it?"

Clara was gazing towards the park, where the shape of the halfpipe cut the air. There was already a gang of Boarders in the middle of the pipe, and approaching it from the West side of the recreation ground was another group of boys.

"That's Rocket's lot," Carver said. "Ah, the Gangs of Greylinghurst," he added sardonically.

"That's not going to be pretty," Jena said dryly. "Come on," she murmured soberly, linking arms with Clara and turning her away, "We should go."

*

Flinn watched Rocket and his gang approach with a cool gaze. He wasn't afraid of the group, but it was reassuring when Ash and the others joined him on the halfpipe, back from their excursion.

"Here we go," Ash muttered dryly as Rocket sauntered up to the rail with his crew crowded round him.

"Wassup Ashley? You don't look pleased to see me," Rocket said with a wolfish grin. He folded his thick arms across his broad chest. Even without the tight T-shirt it would be easy to see that this was someone who spent a lot of time working out in his brother's garage. Rocket was only seventeen, but there was a hardness about his eyes and jaw that made him appear older, and, although he was good-looking with his dark hair and hazel eyes, there was an air of restless energy about him that was unattractive.

Ash eyed him with his characteristically calm expression. "What do you want, Rocket?"

"Do I need a reason to stroll around my home turf?" Rocket returned, a slight challenge in his voice. His neck muscles tensed for a moment and then he laughed shortly. "I heard you had a deve problem. Been letting deves paint your precious halfpipe Ashy-boy?"

Ash just raised an eyebrow, refusing to be baited. He wasn't intimidated by Rocket, and he was too smart to be provoked into an altercation in broad daylight and in the middle of the village. And he had better things to do with his time.

"It's not a problem," he replied flatly, "Nothing a little paint remover can't handle.

Thank you for your concern – I'm touched."

Rocket's grin turned to a snarl and he unfolded his arms, cracking his shoulders and taking a step forward. He was notorious for his short temper and, for a second, Flinn thought he was going to leap over the rail on to the halfpipe. But he didn't. As if he had decided Ash wasn't worth it, he rolled his shoulders back and stood with his feet apart.

"Reckon it's an insider job you've got there, Ashley," he sneered, "One of your boys must be a deve. You wanna sort that out before the Double D get to you."

"Again, thank you for your concern," Ash responded cooly, "Have a nice day."

Rocket gave a shark-toothed grin. "I wouldn't want them getting to you before I do, Ashy. I'll be seeing you real soon."

He turned slowly and strolled away, his gang following after him and exchanging gestures with the Boarders as they went.

Ash let out a long breath after they had gone, and glanced at Flinn.

"Slightly fishing for a fight?" Flinn said.

"He's going to get one, if he carries on like that," Ash replied. He shrugged as if to change the subject and picked up the carrier bag he had brought with him. He took out a can of paint-remover and threw it to Radley. "Let's get this stuff off."

"You know it's probably Rocket who did

this," Radley said, shaking the can and eyeing the artwork with distaste.

"It's not his style," Flinn replied, "He would do something more obvious. And obscene."

"It's probably just some loser's idea of a joke," Ash said with another shrug, "Let's just get it off – before someone *does* decide to call the Double D."

*

Marson opened the flagged folder on his computer for the latest blackwashing, lightly tapping one finger on the desk whilst he scanned the individual documents. Each piece of evidence in the case had been efficiently labelled and saved to the folder as it came in by the data department. There was an unusually high level of evidence for this case. It appeared the history teacher had a particularly large supply of illegal material. He had somehow managed to obtain a wide range of documents, so precisely how and when he had done this would need immediate investigation. If he had gained the material from another deviant then it might lead them to the source. On the other hand, if he had got them from an archive, which was possible considering his professional background, then there was a loophole in the system somewhere which would need identifying and closing up.

Marson moved his finger to scroll through the files and shook his head disapprovingly. He recognised most of these materials: it was the usual stuff deviants seemed to get their hands on - ancient documents that had been out of circulation for so long that their existence had almost become mythical. It was the sheer volume of documents that concerned him. How had one deviant managed to get hold of this many texts? Marson's instinct told him this was just a whiff of greater trouble brewing. This accumulation of illegal material, combined with the steady increase of reports, whispered that The Assembly was growing rapidly. It suggested deviancy was spreading quietly and quickly, like a disease.

The Divinity Division only had one line of defence for that, which was the quick identification of deviants and their subsequent prosecution. They could no longer wait for blackwashing to occur. It was now time for a more active approach if they were going to crush this growth. It would have to be search and detain. Marson wasn't a fan of dramatic clichés, but it was true that after the detaining came the metaphorical destroying. That was the job of the rehabilitation centres. Using the information the Division collected on their deviants, the rehabilitation programme went about systematically breaking down the individuals in their care. It was a necessary process, Marson had to remind himself if he ever experienced a twinge of pity for the subjects; it was the only way of stamping out the deviancy. You couldn't afford to leave even a smouldering flax or it would quickly reignite. The plan was extinction. Belief in divinity needed a strong antidote, or it would return as an epidemic.

But they had to start with searching and Marson had a secret weapon for that.

*

Clara was in the back garden, practising flipping the board as Flinn had shown her, when Carver dropped casually over the fence and stood watching her with his hands in his pockets, chewing on a liquorice bootlace hanging from his mouth.

"Read your letter yet?" he asked when he had finished the lace.

Clara dropped the board on the grass and sat on the swing seat.

"Not yet."

"Lace?" Carver offered, taking the packet from his pocket and holding it out to her.

"Thanks."

He watched as she took one and began

rolling it into a coil. "So you didn't get caught?"

"No."

"No, you didn't get caught? Or no, you did?"

"Both."

"Fine. If you want to have your secrets...," Carver scorned, trying to snatch back the bootlace sweet.

Clara popped it quickly in her mouth and stuck out her tongue. She laughed. "You're so nosey – intercepting my post, giving me the third degree – and following me..."

"You know she'll kill you if she finds out you've started skateboarding," Carver said casually, ignoring the accusations and pushing the board to and fro across the grass with one foot.

"My aunt?"

"Jena." He paused. "Your aunt too."

"Yes," Clara agreed soberly.

"She's got her eye on you," Carver said matter-of-factly.

"Jena?"

"Your aunt. It'll be curfews and rules and netball and boarding school eventually."

Clara laughed. "Why netball?"

"It's always netball," Carver replied with a bafflingly dark tone. "Or hockey, or some other awful team sport."

"Don't be daft. My parents will be back in

three weeks."

He looked alarmed. "I thought they were back next week?"

"They had to extend their stay by two weeks."

"Bummer," Carver said quietly and then purposefully caught her eye, "Did you hear about Mr Summers?"

"Our history teacher?"

"He's been blackwashed - broke the Divinity Laws." Carver watched her closely as he spoke.

Clara's grey eyes glanced away as they clouded over with a hint of some emotion, but it was too brief a flicker to determine her precise reaction to the news. "Which ones?" she asked after a pause, her gaze meeting his again with a startling directness.

Carver hated it when she did that. Clara had an uncanny knack of looking straight into you without letting you get past those quiet grey eyes in return. It was like looking into a one-way mirror. It was a very unsettling experience and made Carver feel exposed, vulnerable and always a little guilty.

He shrugged. "They only mentioned the Law of Witness..."

"Mr Summers," Clara said flatly, "Who would have guessed?"

"You just never know with people,"

Carver agreed, flipping the board and glancing over it, just as Flinn had that morning. "Old board," he observed and then turned and walked with it to the side gate. He propped it in the corner where the fence met the gatepost, hurdled over the gate and disappeared down the drive.

The backdoor opened so suddenly that Clara jumped in surprise.

"We're back," Sandy said, casting a quick look about the garden, "What have you been doing?"

"Not much."

Her aunt nodded slowly as if not entirely convinced. "I'm going to put dinner on," she said. "You can make a salad and lay the table."

"Okay." Clara got up quickly from the swing and walked to the back door. She stopped on the step and glanced towards where Carver had left the board. The end of the house was just obscuring the gate and the corner of the fence, so the board was out of sight from the door. Clara mentally thanked her neighbour and hurried into the house.

The conversation with Carver revolved in her head all afternoon. For some reason, what he had said in jest had stuck in her mind. He was right that her aunt would not be pleased to discover she had taken up skateboarding. Sandy would probably forbid her from skating and confiscate the board. It wasn't that there was anything inherently wrong with skateboarding but Boarders didn't have a good reputation with adults and even their peers, apart from Jena, knew to keep out of their way. Clara had no intention of becoming a Boarder. She doubted her own commitment to learning to skate anyway; she just wanted to try it. There had been something about stepping onto that board at the top of the halfpipe that had made her feel alive and, more significantly, free. Just for a moment, everything else had been left on the tarmac and she wanted that again. She wanted it not to matter that her parents were away, that Mr Summers had been blackwashed, or that she was lonely now her aunt was looking after her.

Clara wondered if Carver was right. Would her aunt start introducing new rules and curfews? It wasn't that Sandy was cruel or neglectful but there was a coldness in her manner and an inclination to suspicion, which Clara didn't seem able to appease in any way. Clara had always been a good girl; she was polite, helpful, obedient and undemanding. But this just seemed to displease her aunt further. She rejected Clara's offers of help and she expressed annoyance when Clara did anything unasked. The steady routine Clara was used to with her parents had been altered to exclude her. Sandy insisted on cooking every meal herself, even when she was not going to be around to eat it (which was frequently the case). She had hired a cleaner to come in once a week and clean the house, and a gardener to cut the lawn and weed the flowerbeds.

Clara was not entirely sure what to do with her extra free time and whatever she did do seemed to draw only disapproving looks from Sandy. If she went out with Jena her aunt would be waiting for her return with questions about where she had been and who with. When she was at home it was clear she was in the way of Sandy's reading, cooking or socialising. Clara often retreated to her room, which was the only place Sandy seemed happy for her to be. If her uncle did not spend so much time away it would be different. But he worked late in the city most days and was often at social functions at the weekends so she hardly saw him. And when he was around Sandy usually whipped him away for herself.

Clara had quickly realised that she would have to get used to spending a lot of time on her own until her parents got back. The one thing she could be grateful for was that, as long as she did not cause any trouble, there would be no interference from her aunt.

If she got caught skateboarding however, that might change.

Everything in her life was finely balanced at the moment. One wobble the wrong way and everything would go skeltering off the edge, just like a skateboard off the top of the halfpipe. And just like that, the experience would be painful.

They were eating dinner when her aunt mentioned Mr Summers.

"Did you hear the news?" she asked, unusually directing her question to Clara, "About the history teacher?"

"Yes."

"Oh." Her aunt sounded a little disappointed.

"Carver told me."

"That boy next door?"

"Yes."

"Well, I can't believe it. To have a deviant so close."

"Very surprising," her uncle agreed mildly.

"Did you know him?"

"Who?" Clara asked in surprise.

"The deviant."

How quickly his name and even occupation were forgotten: reduced from a person to a crime. And because she didn't want to talk about it anymore, Clara lied.

"No."

"You take history, don't you?"

"I don't have him."

"That's something at least," her aunt sighed. "Imagine someone like that teaching children. Teenagers are so impressionable – they'll believe anything."

"Deves are generally considered to be social outcasts – no teenager even wants to be associated with them, let alone listen to what they believe," Clara said simply.

"Deves?" Sandy repeated suspiciously.

"Deviants, darling," her uncle explained, "Kids have to abbreviate everything, you know. Do you still call the Divinity Division the 'Double D'?"

Clara smiled. "Yes."

"We used to call them that too. How's your friend Jena? Did you see her today?"

"Yes. She's gone on holiday now though."

"I didn't know that," Sandy said flatly.

"What will you do now with all that lovely long free summer holiday time you have?" her uncle asked teasingly.

Clara shrugged sheepishly. "Probably hang out with Carver."

"Good, good," her uncle responded, but her aunt made one of her ladylike snorts and gave Clara a look that made her feel unsettled.

I hope Carver's wrong, Clara thought. Please may he be wrong. Otherwise everything would soon be falling into the hard, unforgiving bowl of her world.

*

Whilst the rest of the village was wrapped in a sheet of still night, watched by a sea of stars, the park was alive with light and movement. The rough whirr of wheels punctuated the lively chatter around the halfpipe where two large battery-powered lamps shone from either platform, casting two cold white halos over the group. There were about eight Boarders either skateboarding or spectating.

Flinn stepped over the rail into a circle of light and was hailed loudly by Radley, who lobbed a can of drink at him. Flinn caught it in one hand and jumped on to the halfpipe next to Ash.

"Didn't think you would make it."

"Just for a couple of hours." Flinn opened his drink and glanced at the bare patch on the wall just below the word DEVE. "Do you think Rocket had a point?"

"About what?" Ash asked.

"About the deve graffiti. That it was one of us?"

Ash wrinkled his nose. "Nah. More likely

to be one of Rocket's lot trying to stir up trouble. I don't think any of us would be stupid enough to graffiti our own halfpipe with something like that."

"Except that's exactly the sort of thing a deve might do."

Ash snorted dismissively and glanced round him. "Who do you reckon then?" he said teasingly, "Radley? Marty?"

"Marty?" Flinn raised an eyebrow and laughed. "You should have heard him the other day, ranting on about that deviant teacher – going on about how the penalties weren't tough enough – how perverse deviants are and they ought to be hunted down."

"That's a bit extreme," Ash said, "They're only deluded, not psychopaths. Besides, if it did turn out to be one of us, we wouldn't give them up to the Double D – you don't do that to your kind."

"But they wouldn't be our kind," Flinn said matter-of-factly, "They'd be a deviant."

"I don't see what difference that makes."

"It means we didn't really know them. It means they didn't trust us enough to tell us the truth."

Ash laughed. "Would you?"

Flinn grinned. "This lot? Not as far as I could spit..."

"Which ain't that far!" Ash agreed.

The creak of the park gate suddenly cut the night air. Ash spun round quickly and strode to the park side of the pipe. There was a general jostle in that direction and Flinn slowly put down his can and joined Ash on the edge of the apparatus. He felt Ash tense up beside him as Rocket and his friends crossed the tarmac towards them. From the number of his followers and the way he swaggered in a beeline straight to the pipe, it was clear Rocket had come with one purpose in mind.

"I don't think we're going to avoid it this time," Flinn said dryly to Ash.

"Who says we want to?" Ash replied grimly. He took a deep breath. "Let's get this over with." He stepped confidently off the halfpipe and stood with his hands in his pockets as Rocket stopped just a few feet from him.

"I've come to liven up your party, Ashley." Rocket said sinisterly, coiling a bicycle chain around one fist. He swung the free end gently by his side.

"What exactly do you want, Rocket?" Ash said calmly.

Rocket's lip curled into a snarl. He hated Ashley Morgan. He would never admit it, but he was a little afraid of him. Ash was smarter, younger and a natural leader. He had the admiration and loyalty of his

Boarders, and no one had ever questioned how or why he should be followed. And Rocket feared him for that. Rocket was painfully aware of his own deficiencies, which seemed numerous and insurmountable to him. Any qualities he did have were already surpassed by his older brother, Royce. Rocket knew his gang stuck with him because he was bigger and stronger than them, but even so, they were more afraid of his brother. In fact, even though he would never admit it, Rocket was also afraid of Royce, but he couldn't hate his own brother: he was family; so he hated Ashley Morgan twice as much instead.

What didn't help was that Ash didn't really hate Rocket in return. He just didn't care enough, and his calm, cool manner towards Rocket was more provocative than an insult or angry word. Somehow, Ash Morgan made Rocket feel small and insignificant, like a little boy again. This was made worse by the fact that Ash had not always been this collected. Everyone knew that, up until the age of ten, Ash had been an unstable, out-of-control terror. He had once broken the nose of another child for sitting in his seat. And then one day, for no apparent reason, it stopped. No one knew what, but something happened to make the anger-filled boy rein in his emotions and adopt this calm, collected exterior. This uninterested, level-headedness drove Rocket crazy. Rocket was determined to undermine it by provoking Ash to the same level of frustration he suffered - and then pound him to a pulp with his fists. And that was where Rocket knew he had the advantage. When it came to physical combat, Rocket was bigger, stronger and angrier.

"I want to see you put your fist where your big, arrogant mouth is," he spat sneeringly.

"No," Ash returned calmly, but with a slight edge to his tone, "You want me to put my fist where your mouth is."

"Want to try it, Ashy?" Rocket challenged, enjoying the satisfaction of hearing his gang draw up behind him as he took a step forward.

"I might, if you ditch the bicycle chain," Ash said casually, "Unless you think your fists aren't up for it?"

Rocket laughed, feeling elated by the tension. "I don't care what you say, Ashley," he said, meaning it for once, "I just wanna see you bleed…" and with a lightning movement, he swung the chain upward to slash at Ash's face.

Caught unawares and full on one cheek, Ash stumbled backwards, caught his foot and fell. He was still standing close to the halfpipe and his head hit the concrete with nothing to cushion the impact. The crack of contact pierced the air and brought a momentary silence which was broken only by Rocket's laugh.

Flinn swore and jumped down from the pipe to where Ash was trying to get to his feet. Radley grabbed Ash under the arms and pulled him up. Ash squinted at Flinn through one eye, put his hand to the back of his head and then pulled it away, red with blood. He wobbled a little and put a hand on Flinn's shoulder.

"He's nuts...," he said in surprise, "I'm gonna kill him."

"No. You're not," Flinn hissed, pulling him back, "You're hurt."

"He will kill you, Ash," Radley agreed, "You should get out of here."

Ash looked defiant for a moment, but then his face blanched and he gulped as he started to sway.

"Go!" Flinn hissed, pushing him on to the halfpipe.

Radley pulled Ash up and dragged him to the other side.

Rocket took another step forward, high from his achievement, and suddenly found his way blocked by a wall of Boarders.

"Hiding Ashy-boy?" he called. His gaze switched to the Boarders blocking his path.

"Get out of my way, girls," he snarled and slashed the chain forward again.

This time it connected with Flinn's arm as he grabbed it and pulled it from Rocket's grasp. In one quick movement, he flung it across the park where it slid over the tarmac with a musical jangle.

Rocket eyed Flinn warily. He didn't know much about Flinn Raize, but he was clearly taller and stronger than Ash, and had a confidence that was more threatening than Ash's calm. Flinn's keen blue eyes studied him with the air of one who wasn't afraid or angry: one who had a fixed purpose and wouldn't be diverted.

"You gonna try and make me leave?" Rocket sneered.

"Not going to try," Flinn said simply, "Just going to make you."

Rocket struck out with a fist. Flinn sidestepped and Rocket heard the crack of knuckles on his jaw before he felt the blow. He staggered back, rubbed his jaw and then straightened. Flinn was still looking at him with that cool gaze, arms loose by his side. He'd learned something about Flinn Raize now: he was quick and he had a precise right hook. Here was someone who was clearly a fighter.

The rest of the Boarders stepped forward and Rocket heard his own gang mimic them with low snickers. He grinned. Finally, not only someone who knew how to fight, but someone who *wanted* to fight. This was going to be a satisfying night...

Chapter Three

The park was shabby at the best of times: the once bright colours of the climbing frame were anaemic, the paint flaking like dead skin in places; the chains from which the swings hung were coated with orange rust; and the silver tongue of the slide was dimpled and dented. The whole thing was like an ancient ruin, forgotten and abused by the course of time and generations of children. The tarmac was crisscrossed with faint tracks where pitches and courts had been drawn and re-drawn. There was a bench against the shoulder-high west wall, carved with initials and meaningless slogans, and in one corner, a large black bin stood, twisted where something had struck it several years ago. And then there was the halfpipe: a cheap, unfinished idea shipwrecked on the edge and towering above it all.

In the new morning's light, the park looked less shabby and more as if it were suffering the aftermath of a violent storm. Bits of rubbish were scattered on the tarmac. There was shattered glass at one end of the halfpipe where the mangled corpse of a battery-powered lamp lay abandoned. In the playground itself, the bark was scuffed up and the wheel-less deck of a skateboard was turning slowly on the drunken roundabout.

Clara eyed the scene thoughtfully as she kicked her heels against the wall. It had just turned half past ten.

The gate squealed and a red-hooded figure limped across the park towards her. Flinn pushed back his hood as he stopped in front of the wall where she sat. He looked almost as battered as the park: one eye puffed and blackening round the socket and a gash on his lip which had swollen to give him a temporary leer. One hand pressed against the right side of his chest as he looked up at her.

"Ready?" he asked her casually.

Clara dropped down from the wall, clasping her board, and eyed him carefully. "Yes," she said.

"Tenner." Flinn held out a hand and she noted his grazed knuckles. Clara handed the money over and followed him to the halfpipe.

Flinn held out a hand for her board and then lightly dropped it to the ground. "First thing to learn is how to mount the board." And he casually demonstrated.

Clara watched sceptically. He turned the board expertly and skated back to her. "Try it," he said, pushing the board towards her.

Clara looked doubtfully at the board for a moment and gingerly put one foot on it.

"Further forward," Flinn said simply.

She adjusted her placement and made a feeble attempt at pushing off. At the first hint of movement, her feet instinctively abandoned the deck and found solid ground.

"With a little more conviction," Flinn said, folding his arms with a certain amount of care across his chest.

Clara tried to comply, but it took her at least ten attempts before she managed to get both feet on the board for more than a few seconds.

"Good," Flinn said on her last attempt, "You just need to watch your placement so you've got better balance once you're on the board." He demonstrated again, taking the board smartly across the playground and back again to the halfpipe. He came to a halt, flipping the board up and propping it against the edge as he sat down on the pipe, wincing slightly as he cradled his ribs.

"So that's what the sirens were about last night," Clara commented, standing in front of him with her hands in her pockets.

Flinn gave her a knowing smile which his swollen lip turned into a sneer.

"Was it Rocket?" Clara asked.

"You know Rocket?"

Clara raised her eyebrows. "Everyone knows Rocket Shard and his brother Royce. R.S. is carved into every desk at school."

This time Flinn did sneer. "The infamous Shard brothers." He stood up awkwardly and Clara had to resist her natural inclination to offer a hand. "Royce has mellowed a lot now," Flinn continued, "He runs a motorbike repair shop out of his garage. Rocket however, is certifiably insane. He wants to kill me." His tone was matter-of-fact; he wasn't exaggerating, but he didn't seem too perturbed by it, as if it was merely a mild inconvenience.

"What did you do?"

"Got in the way."

Clara bit her lip as she looked at him. She had an urge to put ice on that swollen gash and bind up his grazed knuckles, an instinct which she assumed she'd inherited from her mother. She didn't ask him if he was okay or if he had gone to hospital to check he hadn't broken a rib. Instead, she picked up her board and held out her other hand. "Thanks."

He looked at her hand with slight bemusement for a second.

"Business right?" she said simply.

He gave her one of his peculiar smiles, which she was finding familiar already, and shook her hand. "Practise," he said.

"Tomorrow?"

"Same time."

Clara gave him a mock salute and turning

on her heel, left the park.

Flinn watched her go and looked down at his hand where the skin was still raw on his knuckles. Clara's skin was not warm, but he felt as if he had conducted all the heat of the sun through her and it was travelling up the rest of his arm. He turned to the halfpipe and clambered onto it with an escaping hiss of pain; he was pretty sure Rocket had cracked at least one of his ribs. If the pain got any worse, he would have to get it checked out.

The gate creaked. Turning round, Flinn was relieved to see Radley and Ash walking towards him. Ash's face was still pale and there was a long, angry welt across one cheek and, where the flesh under the eye had been lashed, it was so puffed-up that the eye was half closed. But he was smiling.

"Looking pretty," Flinn greeted him as they joined him in the bowl of the pipe.

"Speak for yourself," Ash replied. "Good thing the police turned up when they did."

"You still got all your brain cells?"

Ash grinned. "Just about. Radley insisted on dragging me home and sitting with me all night."

"You have to be careful, in case of concussion," Radley said knowledgeably.

"Yeah, but you fell asleep after twenty minutes..."

"I did not!" Radley protested. He turned

to Flinn, changing the subject, "You should not be out on your own."

Flinn raised an eyebrow, hugging the right side of his chest tighter where the pain kept stabbing him with every breath.

"Rocket is out to get you," Radley insisted, wide-eyed. "He caught Marty yesterday after the police turned up and he said if he ever caught you alone he was going to kill you..."

"Shut up Radley," Ash cut in, smacking him on the head. He glanced at Flinn with concern. "Though you should probably keep your head down for a while."

"You're not getting maternal on me, are you Ash?" Flinn said lightly, awkwardly sitting down in the bowl of the pipe.

"You know what Rocket's like - he's settled on you as his next target. Just don't let him catch you on your own."

"Man, you should just give yourself up now," Radley advised, "Otherwise, Rocket's just going to get madder and madder..."

"Yeah, thanks Radley," Ash said pointedly.

"And he'll mash you up real good then... you think your face is bad now..."

"I swear, if you don't shut your mouth... I will shut it for you..."

Flinn let them argue about it between them. He knew Radley was right: another fight with Rocket was inevitable. But Flinn wasn't one to slunk around on the heels of everyone else to avoid trouble. He would meet Rocket, but on his own terms; and maybe he would come off worse, but that was better than living like a hunted animal. He wouldn't be Rocket's prey.

"Have you gotta go soon, or are you free this afternoon?" Ash asked suddenly.

Flinn glanced at his watch. "I'll have to go." He scrambled to his feet, automatically putting an arm round his ribs as he anticipated another stab of pain. But the sharp pinch never came; instead there was just a dull ache around the area.

"You all right?" Ash asked.

Flinn took a deep breath, bracing himself for the delayed sting. An expression of relief, mixed with uncertainty crossed his face. "Yeah," he replied vaguely, "I'm fine."

*

The trial did not take long. It took less than two hours to determine the extent of the deviant's guilt and for the judge to decide on an appropriate sentence: six months in rehabilitation. Of course, he had confessed, as they always did; breaking the third and fifth Divinity Laws. They always broke those two. The Law of Witness was a little precarious; after all, it tended to come down to the say so of one person, and you had to prove that the expression of belief in the divine had been given without invitation. What constituted an invitation to share an expression of belief in the divine was always a point hotly argued by the defence.

Breaking the Law of Communication was easier to prove. If you didn't have the proper documents of authorisation for reading restricted material, then you were guilty. If you had in your possession or had produced anything with illegal content, then there was no doubt about your guilt either. Private ownership of such material or removal of them from the archives was forbidden. Curiously, this was usually the first Divinity Law to be broken. Once deviants had obtained, produced or exchanged such material, they had certainly committed themselves to their deviancy.

That's why, looking over the final reports from this latest trial, Marson was bothered; this was too much material for one deviant to collect on his own. And then there was the other, more disturbing fact: too many texts missing. Marson had checked it three times; the quantity of printed illegal documents, recorded on the deviant's computer, was not equal to the number of hard copies of those illegal documents. In some cases, where two copies of a document had been printed there was only one hard copy recorded in the evidence. In other instances, there were no paper versions of documents that had been reportedly printed from the computer. It was possible that they had been destroyed or lost, but there were too many gaps and too many of these with specific content, for Marson's liking. There was only one explanation that his experience could raise: this was not a lone deviant. There must be another - what they termed a neophyte, a new deviant. The history teacher had turned someone, and then he had supplied them with illegal documents to feed their deviancy. If this was indeed the case, then there was another deviant out there. Someone had slipped under the radar, and had to be found. This neophyte had to be found quickly, before the deviancy spread further.

Marson could think of only one person who could track and catch an unidentified deviant. He would have to call in his secret weapon. He would have to call in Hants.

*

The envelope crackled as Clara prised the flap open with anticipation. The fat folds of paper resisted her tug before pulling free from the paper case they had travelled in halfway across the world to reach her. The sheets were scrawled over in closely written lines of blue ink and left a fine dusting of sand on her fingertips. This was seven days' worth of letter, carefully collated by her parents every day of their first week away. She could picture them in the evenings, after their work at the dig, taking it in turns to write to her about their day: the people they had met; the work they had done; their plans for the next day and what they hoped to find then; and how they wished she and Greg were with them. She had waited a whole week for this letter and she wanted to savour it. It had been hard not just to rip it open the moment Carver had handed it to her yesterday, but she had made herself wait for a private moment, when she wouldn't be interrupted or too distracted to give it her full attention.

Clara let the letter lie on her lap for a moment, her fingers tracing the lines of writing gently, as if they had a life of their own. Taking a breath, she unfolded the sheets and smoothed the top page with one hand. Her father's voice leapt from the page at her: *'Our Darling daughter…'* Immediately, Clara could see him with his shirt sleeves rolled up, his wire-framed glasses on his pointed nose.

'We are so excited to be here. Arrived early in the morning when the temperature was already well into the thirties. The heat sticks to you like glue out here – nothing seems to shift it; not buckets of cold water, iced drinks or the little handheld fans they gave us in our welcome packs. And the dust – that sticks to you too. It gets everywhere. You don't notice it until you wipe your brow with a handkerchief and it comes away yellow-brown with sweat and dirt.

But it is wonderful to be here. You would love it – it's like nowhere you have ever seen before...'

Clara smiled to herself; she was pleased they were happy. It was an opportunity they thought they would never have again, and she was glad they were enjoying it enough to extend their stay another two weeks. Perhaps she would get another letter.

There was a knock on her bedroom door and, before she could answer, Sandy came in. She gave her usual scan of the room, as if she was expecting to see something out of place, before her eyes alighted on Clara, sitting on the window seat.

"What are you doing?" she asked casually.

"Reading Mum and Dad's letter."

"I didn't know that had arrived." She folded her arms and glanced around the room again before continuing. "I was thinking," she said matter-of-factly, "Since your friend is away now, you'll have a bit more time on your hands. You should do something active, so I've signed you up for something at the Sports Centre."

"Oh," Clara said, unsure what to do or say to this. "What is it?"

"Netball. If you don't like it, they also do lacrosse or hockey. A team sport will be good for you – you'll get to meet new people."

"When is it?" Clara asked, trying not to choke on her incredulity as Carver's warning rang through her head.

"Eleven a.m. to noon. They run three sessions a week. There's one tomorrow. I'll take you for it tomorrow, but there's a bus that will take you there and back the rest of the time."

"Oh," Clara said again, "Thanks." She hesitated, her brain trying to figure out this unexpected development. As she had essentially been told she would be going, she was fairly sure that protesting or attempts at negotiation would not be received well. "Are all of these options morning sessions? They don't do afternoon ones...?" she ventured.

"They're all in the morning," Sandy said impatiently, "I don't think an eleven o'clock appointment is going to intrude much on your lie-ins, Clara."

Definitely no room for negotiation then.

Not now, anyway.

"Okay," she responded quietly, "Thank you."

"We will leave here at twenty to eleven tomorrow," was Sandy's parting instruction.

Clara sat and stared at the closed door for a minute, subconsciously tapping her middle finger against her thumb where her right hand rested on the letter. She was supposed to meet Flinn at ten thirty tomorrow. Three mornings of netball, or hockey, or whatever horror Sandy had in store for her, was not going to leave her with many skateboarding lessons a week. Perhaps Flinn could rearrange for the afternoon? It was worth trying. Flinn might be a little easier to negotiate with than Sandy. She would have to see if she could find him before tomorrow morning. It was already late afternoon. Perhaps the Boarders would be in the park again tonight. But then how would she talk to Flinn alone? And if she was going to get out of the house after dark, she would have to sneak out. Clara noticed the tapping on her lap and clenched her fist abruptly. It was worth a try.

*

Overlooked by watching stars, shining like glitter on black paper, the park was still and silent with the inky night. It was the darkest and coldest part of the night, the day's heat having evaporated over the fields on a late breeze. The quiet was disturbed by the wail of the gate turning on its hinges. Cautious steps trod the tarmac and a white shaft of torchlight suddenly stretched through the dark. The steps and the light advanced across the playground until the halfpipe emerged like a ship on the waves of night, lit by the beacon of a lighthouse.

A hooded figure boarded the hull of the pipe and swung the light of the torch onto the wall where 'DEVE' still sat proud from the rest of the graffiti. The figure swung a bag off the shoulder and fumbled inside for a minute. A moment later, a clack-clack sounded across the park, followed by a soft hiss.

Chapter Four

Clara had never been good at either catching or throwing, as she had demonstrated again this morning. The most defining moment had been when she completely failed to catch a pass and had ended up with a netball in her face. Now she remembered why she hated team sports. She was not sure which was worse: the pain or the humiliation. Somehow, it had been more embarrassing than falling off a skateboard in front of a group of Boarders.

She winced inwardly. Flinn would be angry at her. Or would he? She was not sure how he would react to her missing their lesson without warning him. After all, he was already up a tenner. She had tried to find him, managing to get approval for a walk after dinner when it was still light; but there had been no one in the park, though she had hung around long enough to get chastised for staying out too late.

She sighed. She was tired and hot and desperately trying to work out how she could avoid going to netball again. She had to find Flinn before she decided what to do, and then, whatever happened from that, she would have to take things as they came. She wished there was a way around it where she wouldn't have to deceive anybody, but her aunt couldn't know about the skateboarding. Clara knew she was short on time. Everything was going to unravel eventually, but if she could buy herself some more time by not rocking the boat just yet, all the better.

Once she had showered, she pulled on a loose t-shirt and a pair of shorts and walked as quietly as she could down the stairs, wondering if she would be able to leave without drawing any attention.

"Clara?" her aunt called from the kitchen.

Clara hesitated, hoping the call was merely superficial. There was silence and Clara tentatively took another step.

"Lunch!"

Clara crept to the bottom of the steps and tentatively entered the kitchen. She saw that Sandy had laid out a lunch for her at the small wooden table.

"Thanks," she said, easing herself into the chair and feeling her muscles protest at the movement.

Sandy watched her eat half her sandwich before she started packing things into the dishwasher. "Well," she said with an almost forced cheerfulness, "You'll be able to make your own way to netball tomorrow, won't you?" She didn't pause for an answer. "There's a bus that leaves at quarter past ten. It's going to be good for you to meet some girls your own age."

Clara thought of some of the girls this morning, who had looked at her as if she was a tadpole trying to swim with fish, and gave a wry smile.

"They sentenced the deviant yesterday." Sandy said abruptly after an awkward silence. "Six months in Rehabilitation."

Clara tried to swallow the last of her sandwich through the constriction in her throat. "Oh," she managed to respond. She downed her drink and stood up. "What does that mean?"

"What?"

"Rehabilitation - what..." She hesitated and crossed to the dishwasher, "I mean, how do they rehabilitate the person - the deviant?"

"I don't know," Sandy said, appearing to think about it, "They must have certain methods I guess - to correct the deviancy. I know there's a test of some sort that has to be passed before they can be released."

Clara slowly made room for her cup and plate in the dishwasher. "What if they don't pass it?" she asked casually.

"They go through the programme again, I guess."

"What if they never pass the test?"

Sandy snorted, "I doubt that's ever happened."

Clara took a deep breath and tried to keep

her sigh silent. "I suppose not." She shut the door of the machine and quickly changed the subject. "I'm going to walk to the shop – do you need anything?"

"Yes – semi-skimmed milk. Four pints."

"Okay."

"Don't be long."

Clara grabbed her bag from the bannister and slipped on her shoes. "I won't."

The day had turned muggy; the heat was trapped by a band of cloud that was slowly spreading on the horizon like a ripening bruise. By the time Clara reached the shop the humidity was clinging to every inch of her body. She bought the milk and made a detour through the park. A lone figure was sitting on the halfpipe. The leer had gone from his lip, but he watched her approach with cool, blue eyes.

"I'm sorry," was the first thing she said. "Something came up – I tried to find you yesterday."

He watched her quietly as she stood before him, one hand holding the other wrist in front of her, gently swinging the carrier bag against her shins whilst water from her hair soaked into the shoulders of her t-shirt.

"Sorry," she said again, matter-of-factly but with sincerity.

He shrugged. "Your tenner."

"I don't suppose...," she began, and then hesitated, "I don't suppose you can change to afternoons?"

Flinn gave her a mildly curious glance. "I can't do afternoons," he said.

Part of her wanted to ask why, but his demeanour did not invite curiosity, so she said nothing and merely gave him a thoughtful look, as if she had come to an interesting page in a book she was reading. Then her eyes lifted past his shoulder, and she climbed onto the halfpipe behind him. Flinn swivelled round to see her staring at the wall.

"Must have been done last night," he observed.

"Do you think it's Rocket?" Clara asked.

"No," Flinn replied, standing up next to her, "It's an odd thing to do – why change the word DEVE to DIVINE?"

"I don't know," Clara mused quietly. She switched her gaze towards him. "Tomorrow, ten thirty?"

He smiled. "You're not going to stand me up again?"

"Probably not."

"Then don't be late." He jumped down from the halfpipe, leaving her standing in the middle of it and staring thoughtfully at the wall again.

Clara thought of Mr Summers, the mild

mannered, slightly eccentric history teacher. She had never seen anyone so in love with ancient history, except her parents. Whenever he recounted an event to the class, it was as if he had lived it himself. He seemed to have just about every date and its historical importance logged in his memory, ready to recall at will. Clara wondered if some of his eccentricity was a symptom of his deviancy. When they rehabilitated him, would it be corrected out of him? Would he become a different person, less himself and more just an ordinary man with an extensive knowledge of dates and names? She would never know, because she would never see him again. She didn't like thinking about it; perhaps it was best she would not know.

She became aware of the milk bottle, sticking to her leg through the plastic bag. She should get back before Sandy started to wonder what she was up to. At least she had found Flinn. He obviously had his secrets too; he seemed quite emphatic that his afternoons were unavailable, and she wondered why. She had wanted to ask, but his demeanour was so cool and aloof at times that she was afraid of overstepping the boundaries and ruining their arrangement. She had not solved her problem; she was still double-booked and she would have to choose: netball or skateboarding? She told herself as she walked home that she would decide in the morning, but in the back of her mind she already knew what she was going to do.

*

There was a soft knock on Marson's door which he answered with an instant, "Come in!" This had to be Hants. It was exactly four o'clock and Hants was always exactly on time. Marson allowed himself a small sensation of pride as his agent closed the door behind him and crossed the polished floor towards the desk. Hants was his best, the best the Division had, though, as of yet, Marson had managed to keep this fairly secret. He did not like the idea of another section of law enforcement stealing his secret weapon away from him. Hants had been with the Division since he was a young man. Marson was not entirely sure how long this was; Hants had one of those faces that meant he could be aged anywhere between twenty-five and thirty-nine. He had started in the data department of the Division straight from education, passed his agent's exam shortly after and had quickly become a senior field agent. After considerable success on the individual blackwashings, Marson had moved Hants on to the underground movement cases. By rights, Hants was senior enough to be a team leader, with his own group of agents to organise and deploy, but Hants was not the team player type and seemed better employed as a satellite agent, following his own orbit on the outside of the groups but able to communicate with each as and when it was necessary. As Hants seemed to prefer this arrangement, and it meant he was less likely to be noticed and seconded by other sections, Marson was happy to let him continue this way.

Marson signalled him to sit, and eyed him up and down with an inward smile: immaculate as always, expression cool and collected, green eyes watching him patiently, ready for anything. Marson was pretty sure that Hants had never experienced surprise. He had never seen anything except that calm expression on his face: a little steely perhaps, but attentive and purposeful.

"You've looked into the Summers' case as I asked?" Marson started, never one to waste his breath or time on small talk, "Preliminary impression?"

"There is almost certainly an unidentified neophyte," Hants replied, "Either they'll be blackwashed soon now they're on their own, or there's the possibility there is more than one neophyte. I would suggest this is unlikely, but I have looked up any Code

Reds in the area that might have had a point of contact with the convicted deviant."

"Good. And?"

"One Red, sir, with a confirmed point of contact. I can interview them tomorrow if you wish?"

"Certainly." Marson agreed. He knew getting Hants on the case was the right decision. The agent was already one step ahead, and if there was one thing Hants excelled at, it was identifying a neophyte before they had even popped their head out of the woodwork. He seemed to have a knack for the business, an instinct that had never failed yet.

"Right. Make sure your report on the Red gets to me as soon as you've held the interview."

"Yes, sir." Hants stood up smartly, "I'll have it to you by five o'clock tomorrow."

Chapter Five

This was one of the stupidest things Clara had ever done. She seemed to be compiling quite a list of stupid things recently, but this was currently at the top. Her thumb hovered over the red button and she tried to disconnect the rest of her from the digit and its intentions, as if allowing it a mind of its own. If it supressed the button it had nothing to do with her. She saw the sign approaching through the window and her thumb twitched. With a hiss of brakes and a high-pitched strain, the vehicle came slowly to a halt. Clara wobbled her way to the front in time for the doors to open and the bus driver to give her a funny look. Clara knew what he was thinking: she had only got on the bus at the previous stop on the other side of the village, where she had bought a return ticket to the sports centre five miles away.

Clara ignored his look as she stepped off the bus and swung her bag on to one shoulder. It was a beautiful day and she had a ten minute walk ahead of her, so she was going to enjoy it guilt free. She started back on herself, along baked roads shadowed by tangled hedgerows which were alive and buzzing with the contented humming of insects and the bustling of sparrows. Clara stopped to watch one sitting atop a hedge, his feathered chest quivering with his shrill song. For one beautiful moment, it was just her and the sparrow, sharing the sun together. Clara marvelled how something so small and fragile could make such a loud, clear noise. She envied him his little life in the hedgerow: short but very sweet.

Eventually, she dragged herself away from him and trekked on, feeling the skateboard in her bag bump rhythmically against her back. It was all a rather elaborate charade. Clara bit her lip pensively: charade made it sound better than it was. It was a deception, an elaborate but intentional deception. She had a return bus ticket to the sports centre so that there would be no reason for Sandy not to believe that was where she had gone. As long as Clara got home just before one o'clock and no earlier, there was no reason to suspect she had not gone to netball. The only risk to her plan was that Sandy would do something unpredictable, like decide to pick her up from the sports centre, or take a stroll on the village recreation ground.

Clara could feel the snake of guilt twisting inside her. She knew that what she was doing was wrong. She should not be such a coward. She should just tell her aunt the truth and face the consequences. But she was not ready yet. She tried to assuage the guilt with the promise that when her parents were home, she would come clean and tell them everything.

It was with a little trepidation that Clara turned off the lane and on to the path at the lower end of the recreation ground. As she walked up the East side, she could see that the park was empty - the concrete abandoned for the sand and sea breeze at the beach.

The deviant graffiti was still on the wall of the halfpipe and Clara could not resist gazing at it, until Flinn's voice addressed her from the tarmac. "You made it this time?"

She glanced round with a smile. "I've got to get my money's worth."

"Come on then."

She pulled the board out of her rucksack and jumped out of the halfpipe to join him.

"Right," Flinn began, taking the board from her, "Now you can get on the board, you need to be able to steer it and maintain movement."

He demonstrated by skating across the park, turning smoothly at the end and returning to where he had started.

"Okay," Clara agreed sceptically, taking the board back from him.

"Make sure you get your feet in a good position on the board." Flinn said. He gave her one of his smiles. "And don't jump off."

*

The Divinity Division had a colour-code system for deviants. It was a simple but effective way of classing each deviant according to the level at which they were being processed. Greens were active deviants, not yet brought to trial. Usually this meant evidence was still being collected or verified before an arrest could be made. No deviant was Code Green for long. The time between identification and prosecution was usually very short, so there was never usually more than one Green in the system at any one time. In the past, months sometimes passed without a single Green existing on the list.

Once a deviant had been arrested, tried and sentenced, they became a Code Amber: active, but contained. The minimum sentence for an adult deviant was six months and, for a minor, three months; but some deviants could be Amber for up to a year. Once an Amber had been successfully rehabilitated and released back into society, they became Code Red.

You never got off the Deviant List. Once a code Red, you were considered no longer a significant threat. An agent might discreetly check up on you every now and then, but otherwise, you were left to get on with your life as best as you could. However, that was easier in theory than it was in practice. For a start, you could not return to your previous life. Being found guilty of deviancy would more often than not cost an individual their job. Your family, neighbours and friends knew what you had been and knew what you were now. This was the irony. Although believers in the divine were considered foolish, those who had turned their backs on what they had previously professed were despised. Not only had they been weak enough in the first place to indulge in such fancies, but they had then betrayed their beliefs and proven themselves even more weak-minded and weak-willed than before.

Usually, the pressure of having disgraced themselves so considerably forced Reds to move where no one knew them. Most managed to put together some sort of new life for themselves, but often at a cost: the loss of family, friends or a promising career. Living in the constant fear of their past being discovered, or of reverting to their deviancy, many Reds became reclusive. This was enough to ensure they never reoffended and the Division rarely had to worry about or deal with ex-deviants again.

However, there was always one type of deviant that the Division did worry about: Code White.

There were three ways a deviant became Code White. The first was if they could not be rehabilitated. This was rare and not much of a problem, as it simply meant that the individual was incarcerated indefinitely, often in a secure, isolated unit if the deviancy appeared to be potentially contagious.

The second was when a Red reoffended. This was also rare. Agents were sometimes required to assess a Red if they were in an area where another deviancy had occurred. No one liked doing this; it was difficult to be sure and you needed fresh evidence that a Divinity Law had been broken. Hants still got these cases passed on to him whenever they arose because he had a knack for identifying deviants. There was an element of superstition surrounding this, as if he had a sixth sense for recognising deviancy; but the truth was Hants had a pragmatic approach born of experience rather than any special sense.

Hants covered his Slate and glanced across the road at the green front door behind a white picket fence which enclosed a neat square of lawn and immaculate flowerbeds. This was one of those cases. The Red would not be pleased, or hostile most likely, but it had to be done. Hants could not blame Marson for wanting to wrap up this case quickly. Once it was dealt with, they could get back to dealing with the real problem, the third type of Code White: the unidentified, active deviants. These were the lawbreakers they knew existed, whom they knew ran an underground movement of deviants, but whose identities remained a mystery. The truth was that the number of Whites was growing, probably faster than they were able to calculate; and the more deviants who got together, the less chance there was of them being blackwashed.

Hants knew Marson was afraid that if they did not find this neophyte, there was a chance they would slip into the numbers of the unknown White deviants.

Hants got carefully out of the car, Slate under one arm. He straightened his jacket a little, clicked the lock button on the car key and crossed the road to the green-doored house. The gate opened and closed noiselessly and the house appeared empty and silent as he stood on the step. After the bell had trilled throughout the house, he heard the sound of footsteps and a shadow appeared in the decorated glass panel of the front door.

A middle-aged woman, with dark hai,r swept up in an untidy bun and an apron over her summer dress, gave him a smile that slowly faded as she eyed his dark grey suit and formal appearance. Her brown eyes caught his clear gaze and she swallowed softly before asking: "Yes? How may I help you?"

"May I come in, Mrs Hurst?"

She glanced at the badge in his hand and opened the door wider. "Yes," she said tightly.

She led him through a tidy hallway into a bright lounge, where the French doors stood open and the gentlest of breezes was stirring the pale curtains. The room was neat and minimalistic, and smelt of furniture polish. A book stood open on the glass-topped coffee table and a kitchen timer was ticking away next to it.

Hants looked at the woman, with wisps of mouse brown hair falling over her flushed forehead, in her neat little home, and thought how domestically ideal it appeared.

"How can I help you?" she asked again, indicating a seat and standing nervously against a wall so that her shoulder nudged a small painting hanging behind her. She seemed not to notice, her eyes fixed on Hants and one hand squeezing the corner of her apron.

"Is your son in, Mrs Hurst?" Hants asked calmly, standing with his back to the French doors.

"Is it really necessary to speak to him? Can I help you with anything?" she asked hesitantly, "It's been nearly two years – I'd rather not drag anything up for him..."

"I need to speak to your son," Hants stated coolly.

"It's all right, Mum," a voice said from the door to the hall.

Hants glanced across at where a teenage boy stood, with hands in the pockets of his shorts and keen eyes observing him cynically.

"Is this about Mr Summers?" he asked.

"He taught you history?"

"Yes."

"Were you aware of his deviancy?"

The boy smiled wryly. "You think because I was one that I have some sort of deviant radar? No. I had no idea."

Hants uncovered his Slate and placed it on the coffee table. "Have you seen any of this material before?"

The teenager walked slowly over to the table, hands still in his pockets, and peered at the screen as Hants scrolled through the images. He straightened slowly and gave Hants a very direct look.

"Some of them – two years ago," he said matter-of-factly.

"But not since?"

"No." He gave a small smile. "You think there's another deviant."

"Are you aware of anyone who might be

in possession of any of this material, or who had any contact with Mr Summers, who might have been acting suspiciously in any way?"

"No," the boy replied simply, "Like I said, I had no idea he was a deviant anyway. He was just my history teacher – that was it."

Hants examined the boy carefully. Underneath the casual attitude was a hint of hostility. His tone was dry and cynical for his age and, although he gave the impression he was ready to jump to defend his innocence at any moment, he did not have the mannerisms of someone who had something to hide. In addition to this, his answers were very definite and clear. If a deviant was trying to hide anything, they would be much less distinctive in their answers, avoiding telling the truth without telling a direct lie. It was a peculiar trait of deviants that they never directly lied.

Hants covered up his Slate.

"Is that it?" Mrs Hurst asked. "You don't want to search the house or anything?"

"That will be all for now, thank you," Hants replied as she led him back down the hallway to the front door. He glanced past her at the boy before he turned to go. "Thank you, Carver," he said.

Carver did not say anything, but stood

watching with his hands in his pockets until the door closed.

*

Flinn's instructions proved hard to follow. The board seemed to have a mind of its own and Clara could not overcome her instinct to abandon it once it started moving with any speed at all. Flinn watched her patiently for about fifteen minutes without saying anything. Even his face was expressionless whilst he watched her fail over and over and over again.

"You're afraid of falling off," he said eventually, "Try again."

Clara looked unconvinced but did as he said. Her feet were barely on the board however, before Flinn, who had stood stoically up until now, jerked his leg suddenly and kicked the deck out from under her. She landed hard on her backside.

"Ouch!" she exclaimed, more with surprise than pain.

"You're going to have to get used to falling off if you want to skate," Flinn told her without sympathy, "Try again."

She gave him a suspicious look as she got up and positioned the board again, wondering how long he had been waiting to see her fall on her backside. He was obviously not as patient as she thought.

For a second time, he kicked the board out from under her. Clara just caught her balance in time to avoid hitting the tarmac, but he swiftly hooked one foot round her ankle and jerked her leg out from under her. She gave him a resentful and surprised look from the ground.

"I wasn't even on the board!"

Flinn couldn't help but snicker. "I'll keep pushing you over until you stay on that board. Again."

Clara didn't bother dusting herself off and moved the board a safe distance away. She mounted the deck and then swerved as Flinn made a move towards her. The board turned under her feet and then skittered away without her over the playground. She landed on her hip and swore involuntarily.

Flinn gave her a smile. "Better. Again," he said cheerfully, offering her a hand.

She brushed it away. "I'm going to fire you in a minute."

"I guarantee you will hate me by the end of this."

"*Will* hate you?" Clara retorted dryly, limping to retrieve the board and try again.

This time she made it across the park.

"Turn!" Flinn told her as she reached the end, "Turn!"

Clara tried, but soon found herself staring

up at a cloudless sky. "Ow!"

"You leaned back too far," Flinn said, looking down at her.

"Really..?"

"You should lean forward. Come on. You can't lie there all day."

She let him pull her up this time. Her hand lingered in his for a brief few seconds and he noticed her giving him a funny look, her head tilted slightly to one side. She released his hand and the same prickle of heat shimmered up his arm again. Flinn self-consciously put his hand to his ribs, which he hadn't given a second thought to since the morning after they had been given a good kicking by Rocket.

Clara flicked the skateboard over on to its wheels and mounted it without a word. Flinn watched her travel to the end of the park, lean slightly as she neared the wall, and turn in a perfectly smooth arc. He shook his head. What a contradiction; absolutely hopeless one minute, and then, as if a switch had been flicked, perfect the next.

"Better," he said, as she hurtled towards him and then grabbed his arm to stop. He raised an eyebrow as she nearly pulled him off his feet and the board continued past them. "Next time: stopping."

"You mean there's an alternative to falling off?" she asked wryly, brushing the dust off her jeans. She straightened to see Flinn giving her a keen look with those intelligent eyes.

"Tell me to mind my own business if you like," he said calmly, "But don't nice middle class girls have something better to do with their mornings than hanging round a shabby park with a Boarder?"

Clara walked towards the board and flipped it upright before replying. "Such as?"

"Where's your friend? The nosey one who got you into trouble?"

Clara gave a fond smile. "Jena's on holiday."

"Well, don't your parents know you're here, learning to skateboard with a Boarder?"

Like a grey cloud, a sudden sadness shadowed Clara's smile and she stared at the far end of the playground as if looking for someone there. "My parents are away," she said without emotion, "My aunt and uncle are staying while they're away - and they're very busy."

The look passed and when she turned back to him, she just gave a smile and a shrug.

Flinn wanted to ask why this seemed such a sad piece of information. Clara was an enigma to him. On the one hand, she was completely familiar. Her calm manner and reflective grey eyes already seemed a normal part of his daily existence. He had felt the same when he had met his stepfather and when his sister had been born; they were people who had been missing from his life, but then they had slotted into his world as if he had been keeping a space for them without knowing it.

And yet, on the other hand, Clara did not make any sense. Every now and then, something broke through her unfazed manner: a spark of another hidden life, and it was as if he did not know her at all - which was crazy, because he didn't know her: she was just some girl he had met a few days ago. Why should he feel that he knew her well enough to tell that she wasn't being fully herself with him? Yet he still had the persistent feeling that there was something she was hiding, that there was another person underneath with another life he couldn't access.

"Same time tomorrow?" he asked her casually.

"Yes."

Flinn glanced at his watch. He would be just in time. He headed towards the gate, glancing back where Clara had climbed into the halfpipe. It seemed normal to see her standing there, staring at the graffiti as if she had not seen it before. She seemed to have a fascination with the deviant graffiti. Flinn turned away from the park. He had to tell himself that one day he probably wouldn't see her there anymore. She would get bored, move on from this skateboarding phase and things would go back to how they had been. It would happen, for certain. He had to remember that.

*

Hants knocked on Marson's door at four fifty-nine p.m.

"The Red?" was the first thing Marson said to him as he took the offered seat.

"Safe."

"Shame. That would have made things easier." Marson watched the clock tick over to five o'clock with a thoughtful frown. "Time to go to the source," he said, "I'll arrange an interview with Summers."

Hants nodded. "I'd like to return to Greylinghurst, sir. Further investigation in the area might uncover some clues."

"Yes," Marson concurred, "It would be useful to have an agent in the area. I'll get an interview with Summers for tomorrow and then you had better set up base in Greylinghurst and continue things from there." He tapped the top of the desk rhythmically with a finger. "Summers doesn't seem to have had many contacts outside of the school. The police interviewed all of his colleagues and they came up clean - though they might have missed something." Marson looked at Hants soberly. "You know what that means?"

"It's a student," Hants agreed, "I've obtained a list of students Summers taught. I'll start with those."

"Be discreet. I don't want anyone contacted directly until we've got reasonable suspicion. You know what will happen otherwise - we'll start a rumour mill across the entire county and then we'll have our hands full of false reports and accusations. Amongst all the fuss, we'd lose our deviant for sure."

"I understand," Hants said, standing up and straightening his jacket with one deft tug.

"And you're sure about that Red?"

"As sure as it's possible to be. I'll keep a low profile check on him if you wish."

"Yes," Marson nodded, trying to smooth out the furrow in the centre of his brow with two fingers. He had to remind his facial muscles how to flex out of a frown before the furrow softened a little. Marson could not remember how to smile, but he managed to give Hants a straight-lipped look which he hoped conveyed his confidence in his ability to wrap up this case quickly.

Hants gave him a brief nod in return and left Marson sitting alone at his desk, the frown on his brow sweeping back into place like a stretched elastic-band, suddenly released.

*

Clara stopped next door on her way home. Mrs Hurst answered the door with a face that broke into sheer relief when she saw her.

"Clara! How are you, sweetheart?"

"Well, thank you, Mrs Hurst," Clara replied, wondering who Mrs Hurst had been expecting at the door instead. "Is Carver in, please?"

Mrs Hurst hesitated, her brown eyes apologetic. "Yes… but he's not well I'm afraid. I think he's sleeping - probably just a twenty-four hour bug."

"I'm sorry," Clara said, "I hope he feels better soon."

"I'll tell him you popped by. I'm sure he'll be up and about again tomorrow."

"Thank you."

Clara gave Carver's house a thoughtful look over her shoulder before she let herself into her own.

After a shower and lunch, she gathered

herself up on one corner of the window seat in her bedroom and glanced across at Carver's window opposite. Although his window was open, the curtains were closed. He must be really sick. Clara lifted the broken section of the window sill and took out the letter from her parents. She missed them. It was not just because she was used to having them around, or that they had never been away this long before; it was the fact that she needed them. She needed to talk to them. They were the only people who could hear what she had to say in unconditional, all-accepting, unchanging love. She hoped. At least, it was going to come out soon and she would rather she got to tell it to them first.

Clara stared at her father's blue writing on the page and took a slow breath to calm the tremble in her chest. How would it look, she wondered... if she wrote them a letter? What would she say?

'Dear Mum and Dad, I'm...'

What should come first?

'I'm paying a Boarder to teach me to skateboard.'

Not so bad. They would be bemused, but not shocked.

'I'm pretending to go to netball club when I'm really going to the park to skate.'

That was worse. Disapproval. Disappointment, even. They had brought her up to be better than that. Why lie about that any way?

'Because I don't want Sandy to notice…'

What would she notice? What's your excuse for such a deception, Clara?

'Because I don't want her to notice I am changing. It's a classic sign – like they put in the leaflets: a change in habit, hobbies and even personality.'

And the real reason?

Clara bit her lip, her middle finger tapping restlessly against her thumb.

'And I don't want to pretend I'm something other than what I am, anymore. Sandy will forbid me to skate, and that will be one more thing I'm not allowed to be.'

One more thing? This would puzzle them. What are you, Clara? Apart from a lying, deceitful, middle-class village girl pretending to be a Boarder?

Clara exhaled slowly. This is how it would look in the end:

'Dear Mum and Dad,

I am a deviant. In thought. And in action.

I have broken the Divinity Laws and if you don't come home soon, they're going to catch me out.

They're going to find me.

I'll be blackwashed. Just like Mr Summers, they will blackwash me.

They'll send me away.

Please come home soon…or I might not be here when you return.'

Chapter Six

The transformation was gradual, but Clara was starting to look like she belonged on a skateboard. Flinn watched her critically as she negotiated the obstacle course he had set up for her. She had taken to wearing an old pair of jeans to protect her grazed knee and there was a fresh cut on one elbow where she had fallen over the day before. But it was more than that; her body was starting to respond more instinctively to the movement of the board. Clara did not realise it, but she had a natural sense of balance and spatial awareness that meant she learned very quickly, once she had got the basics. Her hair was tied back, so the focus on her face was clear and she was completely absorbed in what she was doing, but without anxiety or fear; in fact, there was a spark of pleasure in those grey eyes.

Flinn was so absorbed watching her that he almost jumped when she addressed him.

"Better?" she asked.

"Better." He agreed.

Perfect, he thought.

He began to collect up the items he had used for the course and Clara helped him pile them up in the middle of the halfpipe.

"Where are the others?" she asked. "I've come every morning for five days now and they've not been here."

"Four days," Flinn corrected. "You missed one, remember?"

"You're like an elephant," she said, rolling her eyes.

"They go down to the beach – there's a bigger skate park there."

"Don't they think it's odd you don't go?"

"They tend to mind their own business," Flinn replied with friendly sarcasm.

"Hint taken." She looked up at the wall of the halfpipe and to the top of the platform, a good foot above her head. "When do I get to skate on this?"

Flinn put his hands in his pockets and gave her an amused smile. "You're not really a nice middle-class village girl, are you? You're just an adrenaline junkie like the rest of us."

She gave him a smile back and then glanced casually towards the field. Her attitude changed instantly. Flinn saw her shoulders tense and the flush of pink in her cheeks drain away. He heard her swear under her breath before she turned her back abruptly on the field.

"What?" he asked.

"My aunt..."

Flinn glanced past her at the tall figure walking along the path from the corner of the recreation ground. He raised an eyebrow. There was nowhere for Clara to go. The park was open to view and even a hurried escape would be spotted in about twenty seconds when the stately figure reached the beginning of the rail. Flinn did not say anything but pulled off his red hoody and handed it to Clara. She slipped it on, pulling the hood over her head. Flinn pushed her on one shoulder.

"Slouch," he said.

He watched as the tall figure passed the halfpipe. She glanced briefly in their direction but chose not to see them. His gaze followed her until she disappeared amongst the houses on the West side of the field and then he turned to Clara. Her middle finger was tapping subconsciously against her thumb on her right hand and Flinn instinctively closed his hand around hers for a moment.

"That will give you away," he said.

She pulled the hood down and let out a slow breath. "Thanks," she said quietly.

"Come on," Flinn said, putting his hands into his pockets in a way that suggested no one was going anywhere until he decided. "Confess."

Clara hesitated. She wanted to brush the whole thing off as a silly overreaction, but there was something about Flinn's open gaze that suggested he would not be fobbed off.

"I'm supposed to be at netball," she told him as objectively as possible, "Three days a week, my aunt thinks I'm at netball club."

"But instead you're here - with me?"

"Yes."

"That's why you didn't come that one morning?"

"Yes."

He did not laugh at her or appear surprised by what she said. Instead, he looked as if he had known all along but had been waiting for her to tell him.

"You don't like netball?" he asked with a slight smile.

"I can't throw. Or catch."

"Yeah," he agreed, "I can believe that."

"Thanks," she said sardonically, but returning his smile.

"So what do you do when you're finished here?"

Clara shrugged. "Hang around until just before one. That's when the bus I'm supposed to be on arrives back. Then I go home."

Flinn smiled almost sympathetically. "You're going to be in so much trouble if your aunt finds out."

"You have no idea."

He gathered up the stuff in the middle of the halfpipe. "Come on!" He put some of it into her arms.

Clara looked puzzled. Flinn's blue eyes met hers and for a moment, Clara had the urge to tell him everything. She longed for the freedom of confession. Having told him about the netball, her other secret weighed even more heavily on her. But she knew there was a difference between admitting she had some rebellious impulses, as everyone else did, and revealing that she had deviated from the law and committed a crime she should be locked away for.

"Lunch?" Flinn invited.

"Yeah," Clara replied quietly, trying to sound more nonchalant than she felt. It had been a lonely few days. She had not seen Carver all this time, and the only company she'd had were her hour-long lessons with Flinn. This casual gesture of friendship was almost overwhelming.

"You might as well keep that on," Flinn said, indicating his hoody: "In case we come across any more of your relatives."

Clara smiled and put the items he had given her into her rucksack with her skateboard.

"Where do you live?" she asked as they climbed over the rail on to the field.

"That way," Flinn replied, nodding to the East side of the village. "But I have to pick something up first."

Clara gave him a sideways look. "Is this

the thing you do every afternoon that means I have to miss netball club?"

"Because you're so sorry you have to miss it," Flinn laughed. "Yes, it is."

They crossed the field and weaved their way through the quieter streets at the southern end of the village. Here the houses were bigger, with large front and back gardens, long-limbed trees growing over the brick walls, their boughs casting welcome shadows over the road. They turned into the driveway of one of these houses, which had its stately black gates set open in welcome and an elegant silver birch in the front lawn from which hung a wooden swing. As they followed the paved driveway up to the door, the sound of children shrieking reached their ears from behind a high wooden gate at the side of the house.

Flinn rang the bell and it sounded majestically in the hallway. There was a rustle of movement on the other side of the stained-glass door, and then it opened and a woman with perfectly coiffed red hair and a soft smile, stood in the doorway.

"She's just getting her hat," the woman said, opening the door wider and glancing back into a wide hallway with a polished wooden floor that led into a spacious reception area, where a small chandelier hung from the ceiling. Clara noticed a row of small shoes of varying styles along one wall, and a row of pegs above that, with various knapsacks, satchels and jumpers hanging on them. There came the sound of footsteps and a girl of about seven, in pink dungarees, a white t-shirt and white scuffed trainers, emerged from a room and took a green satchel from one of the lower pegs.

"Got your hat, Rosie?" the red-headed woman asked.

The girl held up a white sunhat in her fist. "Yes thank you, Mrs Damon," came the polite response.

Rosie came forward and joined them at the front door. She had Flinn's fair hair, wry mouth and air of confidence, but when she raised her eyes up at Clara, they were large and soft brown, full of a rather serious gentleness.

"Ready," she said to Flinn, offering him her hand. "Bye, Mrs Damon." she called over her shoulder.

When they got to the end of the driveway, she stopped, looked at Clara and then looked at Flinn expectantly.

Flinn smiled. "This is Clara," he said simply. He looked at Clara. "This is my sister, Rosie."

"Hi," Rosie said.

"Hey," Clara returned.

"You look better in that than Flinn does,"

Rosie said, pointing to the hoody.

"Thanks."

They walked back along the quiet lanes, Rosie holding Flinn's hand, but her attention fixed on Clara.

"Can you skate?"

"A little."

"Me too. Is Flinn teaching you? He's teaching me. I've got my own skateboard. Have you got your own skateboard?"

"It's my brother's."

"Is he older? Does he skate too?"

"I should have warned you that you would get the third degree," Flinn said over Rosie's head.

Rosie laughed and shone Clara a bright smile before turning to Flinn. "Do I have to hold your hand?"

"Yes."

"Why?"

"Because that's the rule."

"It's a stupid rule," Rosie said gravely. She sighed like a true martyr and then brightened again instantly. "Is Clara coming for lunch?"

"That's the plan."

"Can I make the sandwiches?"

"Sure." Flinn looked across at Clara with a raised eyebrow. "I hope you like jam in your sandwiches."

Flinn and Rosie lived in a narrow red-brick semi-detached house in a long line of identical buildings. Outside it looked cold and generic, but inside there was a strong sense of a female, homely presence stamped on every room, from flower-patterned cushions on the sofa to a heart-shaped mirror in the hall, and ornaments of tiny birds on the mantelpiece. There was the odd indication that men lived here too: heavy black boots by the back door, which were too big to belong to Flinn, and a football in the hall.

Clara sat at the kitchen table whilst Rosie dolloped jam into each sandwich as Flinn buttered and passed her slices of bread.

"Right, wash your hands," he instructed as Rosie squashed the last slice with sticky palms on to the blob of jam and it squeezed out the edges a little. Flinn frowned at the lid of the jam jar, covered in sticky fingerprints, and gingerly screwed it into place.

"I can't reach," Rosie stated, standing under the sink and waving her hands in the air.

Clara automatically got up, pushed her chair against the sink, lifted Rosie onto the seat and turned on the tap for her.

"Thank you!" Rosie sang as she put her hands under the running water and then reached for the soap.

Clara glanced over her shoulder to catch Flinn watching them with a funny look. He turned away quickly, clearing the butter and jam into the fridge.

"Finished," Rosie said.

Flinn joined them at the sink with a towel and they both watched Rosie dry her hands as if they had never seen it done before. Rosie looked from one to the other in bemusement when she had finished and then flung the towel in Flinn's face.

"Hey!" he exclaimed in surprise as she giggled against him and then put her arms around his neck. She lifted her feet off the chair and hung from his neck as he carried her over to the table like she was a baby monkey. He dropped her onto a chair and slid a plate with a jam-oozing sandwich on it towards her. She tucked in straight away, jam escaping on to the plate, which she stopped to scoop up with her fingers before taking another bite.

They ate in silence, but it was a silence of contentment and companionship that did not need to be filled with teasing or small talk. The silence made Clara homesick for her family. She missed Greg and her parents and the silly little interaction over everyday, mundane tasks. She missed just sitting and enjoying silences like this, where nobody needed to talk because there was no hurry, just the communion of sharing the space together. She had missed belonging to that closeness and now she had been invited to share it again in the most unexpected place.

After lunch, and after she had promised Rosie she would return soon, Clara walked back through the village feeling that her burden was a little lighter. For a few hours, she had felt normal again: in a family environment where she had been accepted as she was and had forgotten the terrible secret she was keeping. As she neared her own home however, it began to weigh on her again. Home was not home anymore, not without her parents. She felt like an intruder in hostile territory, surrounded by suspicion and danger, and having to pretend to be something she was not; or rather, pretend she was not something she was.

It was only when she reached the top of her road that she realised she was still wearing Flinn's hoody. She stopped to peel it off and put it in her rucksack. To her relief, she found there was no one at home when she let herself in, though she checked every room and the garden to be sure. When she trekked back up to her room, she found Carver waving to her from his window.

Clara knelt on the seat and leant out of the window with a relieved smile. "Carver!"

"Hey skater-girl."

"Are you all right?" she asked with genuine concern, "Your mum said you weren't well."

"Just a bug;" he replied with a dismissive shrug, "Thought I'd better come back to the real world and see what trouble you've got yourself into without me."

"No trouble," Clara protested.

"Been going to netball then?" He raised an eyebrow at her hesitation. "Thought not."

Clara shrugged, unable to think of a response to that.

"Don't suppose you've had much chance to practise, with Sandy around?"

"No…" she agreed slowly.

"Well, I know a place we can go."

"Really?"

"Don't sound so suspicious. It's perfectly safe. No one will see you and we won't be breaking any laws - really. Meet you outside in five." And without waiting for her opinion or agreement, he shut the window and disappeared from view.

Clara shut her own window and looked around her room, sensing the emptiness of the house. She sighed and then with a shrug, grabbed her rucksack and headed to the front door.

Carver was waiting outside the gate. "Let's go!"

As they walked out to the farthest parts of the village, Carver was unusually chatty. He wanted to know all about her lessons with Flinn, the letter her parents had written and whether she had heard from Greg. Clara found he was disarmingly easy to talk to when he dropped his cynicism and slightly snide remarks. He seemed genuinely interested in what she had been doing, and Clara detected a hint of what might have been brotherly concern, particularly about her aunt.

Clara was so caught up in conversation that she lost track of where they were walking, so when they turned off the little shaded road they had been on, she had no idea where they were. They must be on the outskirts of Greylinghurst, as there was nothing but fields in any direction and they had not seen a vehicle of any sort for half a mile. The track they had turned on to was dry and crumbly, and took them out of the coolness of the tree-lined road and into the baking sun. There was nothing but the buzz of insects in the long grass, the lazy rustle of birds in the trees and the crunch of their own feet over the broken, dry earth. They were stopped at the end of the track by a metal gate, next to which was a stile, with the painted arrow indicating a public footpath fading on the post.

They clambered over the stile, one at a time, into the field beyond. The grasses stretched away into the distance to meet a line of trees and the blue sky domed over the view like a large silk canopy, with only a single buzzard wheeling beneath it. On the left side of the field was a large structure with four hollow sides and a rusting corrugated roof.

Carver led the way towards the barn and, as they approached, Clara saw that the grass gave way to a large area of concrete, broken up like a jigsaw puzzle, with tufts of grass, brambles and tree saplings growing in the gaps between the pieces.

"It's a bit rough," Carver said, "But no one comes here."

"Was it a farm?"

"I think so – used to be other buildings once, but they're gone now."

"How did you find it?"

Carver shrugged. "Dunno. Come on then – let's see what you can do."

Clara showed him what Flinn had taught her, and Carver's jeering expression returned for a while until she challenged him to do better. Eventually, they just sat on the baking concrete, their legs outstretched in front of them, watching the buzzard circling over the field like a kite without a string.

"You know Mr Summers...," Carver said suddenly.

"Yes...," Clara replied softly.

"Do you think he ever...," Carver hesitated and made a face as if he had something sour in his mouth, "You know... *turned* anyone?"

"Turned them?"

"Into a deviant. Got them to believe what he believed – in a divinity."

Clara shrugged. "Maybe. Why?" She glanced at him to find his eyes fixed intently on her.

"Do you think he did?" Carver asked again.

Clara repeated her shrug. "Why?"

Carver looked out across the field again. "I've heard rumours."

"That Mr Summers turned someone?"

He nodded slowly.

Clara stared ahead of her and tried to remain still. She could hear her heart beating and was sure, if she looked down, she would see its pounding rhythm against her t-shirt.

"Wouldn't they have caught them, if there was someone?" she asked casually.

"Not if they'd been very careful. The Double D would never get anything from Summers."

"Do you think there's one?" Clara asked. "Another deviant?"

"I think there's graffiti on the halfpipe."

"Not anymore." Clara corrected, "I thought that was just someone winding up the Boarders."

"I think it was a message," Carver responded enigmatically.

It was Clara's turn to look at him intently. "What's the message?"

He seemed to notice her gaze before he answered and shrugged expansively. "I dunno. I need an ice cream."

"That's the message?" Clara teased.

Carver snorted and stood up. Clara followed his example, scooping up the skateboard into her rucksack.

"You should ride it back," Carver suggested.

"Yes, of course," Clara replied sardonically, "'Hello Aunt Sandy - would you like to have a go at skating too?'"

"Fair enough. Now, come on - you owe me an ice cream - or two!"

They picked up ice creams from the shop and ate them on the wall outside Clara's house before parting ways. Before he left, Carver gave her an unusually serious look and said: "Just be careful, yeah?"

Clara tried to appear amused, but his demeanour unsettled her slightly. "About what?"

"Just, you know, who to trust - Flinn,

Sandy, Jena – just be careful."

"Okay," she promised, puzzled by his concern.

He gave her an awkward smile and backed towards his house. "It'll be all right," he added confidently, his tone lightening again, "In the end. It'll be all right." and he disappeared into his house, leaving her a little confused.

Chapter Seven

Hants enjoyed this part of his job the most. If anyone had asked him if he loved his job, he would not have said yes. He might have said he believed in what he did, that he knew it to be important in upholding the values of society; he might even have admitted he got a lot of satisfaction from it, but that was because he was so good at it. It was true that he did seem to have a sixth sense for detecting deviants, but he would not have said that he particularly loved it: except for this one part.

The truth was Hants enjoyed a good chase. He enjoyed the process of tracking down a deviant, identifying them and collecting the evidence to convict them. He enjoyed the cat and mouse game, trying to get one step ahead so that he could be waiting by the trap when it was sprung. Other agents hated it. They could not seem to get the hang of predicting how a deviant might move or act. Instead, they preferred to wait for the inevitable blackwashing and collect the evidence after the crime had already been committed and discovered. Hants liked to catch a deviant in the act, at the very moment an innocent thought in the mind became a broken Divinity Law. That was why Marson assigned him to the underground movement cases, where they had no choice but to hunt out and catch deviants.

The trick was to get inside the deviant's head. Deviants were not all the same, however, so this was not an easy task. Because they were usually isolated cases, there were no firm patterns to follow, no official profiles to apply; you had to make a few educated guesses about your deviant and then try to get inside their head and figure out what you would do in their shoes.

This deviant, for example, was a teenager, living in a village community. Of that much, Hants was certain. His interview with Summers had confirmed that. Not that the deviant had told him anything, but Hants knew how to read what he did not say. He was always amused by the surprise the newer agents expressed after meeting a deviant for the first time. The same comment was always made: but he was so ordinary; he reminded me of my uncle; she seemed so harmless; he looked like the guy who fixed my boiler last week.

Of course they were ordinary. They were just people. They probably did not think that what they had done was wrong. Illegal? Yes. Wrong? Not in their opinion. But that did not matter. They had broken the law, and in the eyes of the law they were dangerous, even if they did not look it. These people spread ideas, and ideas can't be stopped easily, once they are out, they cannot be taken back. It did not matter if the idea was initially rejected, it had been entertained and so its ghost would remain, and somewhere, sometime, be resurrected and passed on again.

Hants would not have given Summers a second glance in the supermarket if he had seen him. He was merely a middle-aged man who had spent more time with books than outside in the fresh air, exercising. He had a crumpled look to him, like a piece of paper that had been screwed up and would not spread flat again. Even his standard issue, fluorescent-yellow trousers and jacket looked as if they had been fought over by a pair of dogs before he put them on. The sleeves were overstretched and hung loosely over his hands, and the jacket buttons strained against his paunch stomach. He looked uncomfortable. His mouse brown hair was greying around the sides and he had deep creases at the corners of his eyes from squinting at small printed texts for too long.

When Summers sat opposite Hants at the rectangular plastic table, he sat as if perched on a log and pressed his hands between his knees so that his shoulders hunched slightly.

He did not raise his head, but peered up at Hants from his slightly stooped position, which made Hants feel he was talking to someone who was too far away to properly engage with. He did not say anything, but looked up at Hants with mild eyes, waiting to be spoken to.

In his typical style, Hants got straight to the point, pushing his Slate forward with the illegal material displayed on the screen.

"You produced hard copies of these. What did you do with them?"

Summers squinted at the screen, then took a pair of spectacles out of the top pocket of his jacket and put them on before resuming his contained sitting position.

"I put them in a collection point."

"Where was this collection point?"

Summers gave him what was almost a kind, if not apologetic, smile, but did not answer the question. Hants knew better than to waste time trying to get the answer out of him now; he would make sure the question went on the Exit Test. If he was successfully rehabilitated, then Summers would give them the answer eventually.

"What was the purpose of putting these materials in the collection point?"

"For them to be collected?" came the simple answer.

"By whom?"

"By anyone who wanted them or found them."

"You had a specific person in mind?"

"Perhaps."

"Did this person collect these materials?"

Summers shrugged.

"Who was this person you expected to collect this material?"

The apologetic smile again, of course.

That was all Hants needed to confirm there *was* another deviant and that they were a student. There would be no need for a collection point if it was an adult. Summers could have passed anything on to an adult without raising suspicion. That would not be possible with a student. They were more vulnerable, their property was less private and their time more public. A collection point made sense as the safest way to pass on material. That narrowed the field of suspects to just over two hundred students whom Summers had direct contact with in the school and who could be their deviant. Out of those numbers, eighty-seven lived in Greylinghurst.

This was why Hants had spent the past two days in the village, becoming acquainted with its layout and the routine of the community. He had the residencies of the eighty-seven students mapped out. He had the data on every student who'd had contact with the history teacher checked over the last six months since Summers had started working at the school. Apart from flagging up the Red he had already interviewed, nothing of significance had been found.

But Hants knew the deviant was hidden somewhere in this community. He might well have walked past them already on the recreation ground. He had been confident it would only be a matter of time before some indication of the deviant's presence came to light, and now, it had. Hants stood in the middle of the halfpipe with his hands linked behind his back, and stared at the words painted on the wall: Divine Deve.

'Divine' had not been there yesterday when he had passed by in the afternoon, so it must have been done during the night. If it had just been the second word, he would have thought nothing of it: 'deve' was a common curse word amongst certain groups of young people; it was just one of many expletives to be found graffitied on public property. It was the first word that made the difference. Not even Boarders would write 'Divine' on anything, especially not their own halfpipe. So it was doubtful one of the skateboarders was the deviant. That would be too close to home. Hants was bemused. It was such a public place to put such a message, it was clear the deviant wanted others to see it. The deviant might not want to be found, but did want everyone to know they existed.

His phone buzzed against his chest in his jacket pocket and, without taking his eyes off the graffiti, Hants pulled it out and flipped it open. "Yes?"

He stared patiently ahead whilst the agent on the other end convey a message. His face tightened slightly with annoyance. "Yes," he said again, tersely. "Thank you." And he hung up.

Hants flipped the phone open again and held it up so the wall appeared on the screen. He snapped a couple of shots of the graffiti and then, turning abruptly, left the halfpipe and the park.

*

"Really? Again?" Flinn said as he climbed onto the halfpipe next to Clara. They both stared at the graffiti for a moment in silence.

"It's actually pretty good," Flinn said eventually, "I hope it's worth it."

"What?" Clara asked, distractedly.

"The black eye they'll get if we catch them."

"I doubt that's the cost they'll be most concerned with," Clara replied dryly, turning away and taking the skateboard from her rucksack.

"Do I detect a hint of scorn?" Flinn laughed.

Clara coloured slightly. "No. I just mean, there's a bit more at stake, I imagine."

"True," Flinn agreed, "Which is why I don't get why they run the risk."

"Carver thinks it's a message," Clara said vaguely, holding the skateboard in one hand and looking at the wall again.

"Who's Carver?"

"My neighbour."

"What's the message?"

Clara shrugged. "He didn't say. When do I get to skate on this?" She tapped her foot on the floor of the halfpipe.

"When I say you're ready," Flinn replied bluntly.

"Yes, boss," she responded with a cynical salute.

Flinn smiled and turned to the playground. Rocket was standing on the tarmac with a group of four other boys, who all had silly, smug grins on their faces. Rocket himself was not a silly sight. He was wearing a distressed leather jacket and his usual tight-fitting t-shirt. There was a shadow of a bruise on his jaw and he'd had his hair cropped so that the run of a deep cut could be seen slicing into his hairline from his forehead. He was gently flexing his fists by his side.

"Flinn-boy," he said, with his shark smile fixed on his face, "At last. Have you been avoiding me?"

"Do I look like I've been avoiding you?" Flinn returned contemptuously, glancing round at the open park.

"I've been looking to catch you alone," Rocket continued. "Foolish of you to be out on your own. Very foolish."

"You can't have been looking very hard," Flinn said, "I've been here most mornings."

Rocket chuckled patiently and cracked his shoulders as he rolled them back, warming up. "I'm going to enjoy this," he sighed, taking a step forward.

Flinn felt Clara's arm brush his as she stepped forward.

"Not today," she said calmly.

The mean hazel eyes moved slowly towards her and looked her carefully up and down. For a moment, a look of puzzlement crossed Rocket's face and then, seeing this was nothing more than a slight, gentle-voiced girl, his facial muscles relaxed into a jeer.

"So this is what you've been up to, Flinn," Rocket said, without taking his eyes off Clara. "You should tell your girlfriend to stay out of our business." His tone was patronising. "You obviously know who I am, girly, so you'll know the best thing for you to do is go your way and pretend you were never here. Flinn and I have unfinished business."

"I do know who you are," Clara agreed with a quiet assured tone Flinn had not heard her use before, "Which is why, in less than a minute, when I scream the rec down and the people from the houses over there and the shoppers from the parade come running, I'll be able to tell them exactly who made me scream."

Rocket snorted defiantly, "Go home, girly!"

"I'm not moving," Clara replied plainly, "It's broad daylight, we're in the middle of the village - and I *will* scream if you come a step closer."

Rocket looked carefully at her again, reassessing his initial impression. Her gentle voice had disguised her true intent, which he now saw was apparent in her grey eyes. He had never seen such stone-grey eyes, and, like stone, they betrayed no emotion. Instead, he could feel that frank stare cutting into his own mask, threatening to expose his vulnerability as nothing more than a bully. Rocket felt he was being read, and he did not like it. He preferred Flinn's cool confidence and simple response: an eye for an eye and a tooth for a tooth. This threat was different. He did not know this girl, so he did not know if she would do as she said. If she did, then Rocket did not want that sort of public attention.

"I'm disappointed, Flinn," he said eventually, trying not to sound as if he was backing down, "I never thought you would hide behind a girl."

"I never thought you'd be afraid of one," Flinn said casually.

Rocket snarled, but stepped back with a nasty look at both of them. "I will finish you, Flinn," he promised and then pointed a finger at Clara, "And don't think I won't repay you for your little brave act one day, girly." Then he turned and stalked out of the park with his friends.

Clara watched him go, surprised by her own bravado. She waited for the rush of fear to kick in, but it did not come, just a feeling of anticlimax. Next to her, Flinn's hand closed gently round her wrist.

"Thanks," he said.

"No problem." She gave a half smile: "Besides, he was eating in on my time." She dug into her pocket with her other hand and held out a tenner. "Pay day."

Flinn smiled and took it with a suggestion of reluctance.

"You don't make any sense," he told her,

releasing his hold on her wrist and jumping onto the tarmac.

"Why?"

"Because you're petrified your aunt will find out about you skateboarding, but you're not afraid of pissing off Rocket Shard - who, if he had the chance, would break your legs for challenging him."

"You haven't met my aunt!"

Flinn smiled as she jumped down next to him.

"I've got to pick up Rosie from Mrs Damon's today, if you don't mind jam sandwiches for lunch again."

"I love jam sandwiches."

"After the fifth time in a row you won't," he said.

Clara put down her board and skated off across the playground. She smiled to herself at the implied extended lunch invitation. She was not sure if what Flinn and she had was a conventional friendship, but it had become something that was beneficial to them both. Like Carver, Flinn was easy to talk to and he did not make any assumptions about her based on her gender or background. Unlike Carver, he talked easily; he did not seem to hold anything back. He was straightforward and open in a way that Carver seemed unable to be, and because of that it was easy to be herself with him. Too easy;

dangerously easy. Clara therefore had to concentrate much more on what she said or did, with Flinn because it would be too easy to say something that would give everything away.

She wanted to tell Flinn and she wanted to tell Carver. She felt she owed it to them. They deserved to know what she really was. But she did not want to risk losing them. As much as she trusted both, there was no point in pretending that they would accept her secret without changing their opinion of her. Instead, both friendships, different as they were, had become further reasons not to get caught. Not yet.

"Right," Flinn said matter-of-factly, when he was satisfied she had mastered the basics of riding a skateboard on the flat, "I'm going to teach you the ollie. It's the most basic but essential trick - you need it to do pretty much any skateboarding trick."

He casually demonstrated it to her. To Clara, it looked as if he had jumped in the air and then landed a few feet later with the board still attached to his soles the entire time. It looked impossible.

Flinn smiled at Clara's pensive expression. "You can manage it," he said encouragingly. He manoeuvred himself next to her on his board. "Right - your foot position is really important. You want to put your front foot in the middle and your back foot on the tail… That's right."

He stepped off his board to watch her better.

"Now bend your knees. It's important you bend your knees – especially when you land out of the ollie – or you can bust them pretty badly."

"Great."

"Okay. Now your knees are bent, you push the tail down to the ground. That's right."

"Now what?"

Flinn gave her one of his smiles, both teasing and encouraging at the same time. "This is the hard part. The moment the tail touches the ground, you have to jump."

"How do I get the board to jump with me?"

"You will. Trust me. The tail drop is like a spring – the board will go with you – but you have to move your feet to keep it with you. Like this." Flinn demonstrated again.

"What did you do?"

"Once you're in the air, slide your front foot up to the truck bolts at the front of the board – here. It'll level the board out again. When you land, make sure your feet are over the truck bolts – and bend your knees."

"Right," Clara said without much conviction.

"You just have to give it a go. It'll take a couple of tries."

"A couple?" she repeated, "Feeling optimistic today then?

"Less backchat - more practice," Flinn said.

Clara took a deep breath, ran Flinn's instructions through her head and tried to follow them. Flinn was right, it was jumping when the tail hit the ground that was the hardest part. It took her several attempts and then she forgot to slide her foot over the front trucks. When she finally got it, she could not quite believe she had pulled it off, and Flinn had to confirm with a laugh that she had in fact done it right. And then there was elation, like she had never felt before, as she was able to repeat the trick.

Flinn was amused by Clara's excitement. "Rosie was less excited when she learnt to do that."

"I like your sister," Clara said as she packed up.

"She's not bad is she?"

"How long have you been teaching her?"

"About a year. You got a sister - or is it just your brother?"

"Just Greg."

"And it's his skateboard?"

"Yes."

"Didn't want to teach you?"

"It was a short-lived affair," Clara laughed, "Greg couldn't seem to stick at anything other than chess. I think he was trying to ditch his nerdish image."

"Did he succeed?"

"I don't know. Maybe a little." They started walking across the field and, as Clara spoke, a soft, fond look came into her grey eyes. "Greg's incredibly smart. He was put up a year in school, so he took all of his exams early. He was popular at school too – despite being nerdy. He graduated with a double first and everyone thought he would take some big job in the city. Instead, he got a position with a small charity, earning a pittance and being sent all over the world reviewing their projects. Seems to love it though."

"You get on well?"

"I miss him."

"Are you alike?"

Clara thought for a moment. "I don't know. In some ways. In some ways, not. Greg's more…" She hesitated trying to find a word or phrase that would explain what she meant. "He's more… just more… than me."

"What does that mean?" Flinn asked with a raised eyebrow.

Clara shrugged. "He's more fun and friendly. Smarter, funny and really likeable."

"That's just a big brother thing," Flinn said

dismissively, "We're just older and better."

"Yeah? Well, we'll see what Rosie says about that..."

Rosie's sandwiches were oozing even more than before with sticky red jam, and this time she made Clara watch her skateboarding trick out on the street before she left. It looked a lot like the ollie, except that she turned the board 180 degrees before landing. She explained knowledgeably that it was called a 'pop shove-it' and that it would probably be next on Clara's list of tricks to learn. Flinn rolled his eyes, but patted Rosie affectionately on the head as he sent her indoors to tidy her room.

Clara slung her rucksack on her back and brushed imaginary dust from her jeans. Flinn stood in the front door, leaning against the frame with his hands in his pockets. He gave her one of those looks that Carver always seemed to be giving her now: a thinly veiled concern that did not know quite how to express itself, because it issued from a gut instinct rather than a tangible danger.

"You should tell your aunt," he said, trying to sound casual, "That you don't want to go to netball."

"You just want to take my tenner and not have to give me any more lessons," Clara said jokingly as she began to walk backwards up the road.

Flinn smiled, but the concern did not leave his bright blue eyes, and Clara had to turn away quickly, before the look frightened her too much to go home. Flinn was right. She knew he was right. He probably just thought she should stand up for herself, but it was not just that. Clara was tired of lying, and it would be one less thing to lie about. She wanted to be the good, honest girl she had been before all this. It probably would not be a pretty conversation, but she was going to have to get used to eliciting anger from people, so she might as well take the first hit now. Besides, it was only temporary. Her parents would be back soon, and then it would not matter what her aunt thought, said or did to her.

But she did not feel great about it. She wanted Greg. She needed him. He was always cheerfully sensible, and seeing Flinn with Rosie had made her miss him all the more. Greg would know what to do. She would ask him.

*

Hants stopped off at the Greylinghurst recreation ground before heading back to his Bed & Breakfast. He had spent most of the day at the local police station, which had got wind of the fact that the Divinity Division had visited Summers. One of the Detective Chief Inspector's was now insisting that he should be informed if there was any investigation on a case that he considered to be closed.

Hants hated dealing with the police. Technically, he did not have to speak to them. He could ignore them, flash his badge and get on with his business, but it was an unwritten rule of courtesy that the Division work alongside the regular law enforcement agency as much as possible, to avoid bad feeling and awkwardness in future cases. Hants saw the courtesy as rather one sided; and it did not seem to do much to lessen the bad feeling largely put his way, whenever he walked into a police station.

This DCI he was summoned to deal with seemed to have a general attitude of scorn towards deviants, the Summers' case and Hants in particular.

"I don't see what you people are getting flustered about," he snorted, not looking at Hants but at the various items on his desk - as if they were a puzzle he intended to solve. "We caught the deviant. He's serving six months in some hole of a rehab camp. There isn't anything more to the case."

Hants did not reply, but watched as the

DCI rearranged the items on his desk with subconscious precision that suggested, despite his personal appearance, a certain obsession with orderliness.

"The material 'missing' was probably destroyed by the deviant," he continued, carefully straightening the nameplate, which said DCI Woodward on scratched metal, with painful care, "You know how crafty these bastards can be." He paused with an amused eye. "Though this one wasn't as crafty as he thought. Imagine being blackwashed by a student…"

As if he had suddenly noticed that the conversation had been entirely one-sided and that he had been overly absorbed in aligning the items on his desk, the DCI folded his hands in front of him and looked up at Hants. "What is it exactly, that you have been sent here to do?"

Hants perceived from the emphasis on the word 'sent' that DCI Woodward was under a misapprehension that Hants was a junior agent. He obviously thought Hants was on a petty errand for what was generally, and rather ignorantly, thought to be an unnecessary division. Now it was time to correct him. Hants was very practised at this. It was true that most people were fooled by his youthful appearance into thinking he was inexperienced, and therefore easily dismissed; but once he spoke to them, they never made that mistake again.

"There is a deviant operating right under your nose in the village of Greylinghurst. They have, for some months now, been collecting illegal material left by the convicted deviant, Summers, from an as-yet, undetected collection point. There is every possibility the deviant will pass these documents on to others through similar collection points. We know that the deviant is increasing in confidence and activity because of deviant graffiti in the area, which is quite likely an attempt to contact other deviants or potential neophytes in the area.

We intend to find this deviant before the deviancy escalates and you have your very own underground movement on your hands, most likely an active cell of The Assembly."

Hants delivered his answer distinctly, without a single hesitation or pause for breath, and with a steely eye.

Woodward sat and looked at him afterwards for a moment, folding his thumbs alternately one on top of the other.

"I see," he said eventually, indicating that he saw Hants was not as he first appeared, rather than that he appreciated the seriousness of the situation. "And how do you propose to find this new deviant? Do we know anything more about him?"

Hants noted the change of pronoun from 'you' to 'we', which implied the DCI's reluctant compliance with the investigation. Hants hoped that police cooperation meant they would stay out of it and let him get on with his business. He hoped he would not have to call on them to provide squad cars and armed officers, but it was impossible to know for sure.

"The deviant is aged between eleven and seventeen, an inhabitant of Greylinghurst village and attends the local senior school."

Woodward could not help but scoff, though he immediately tried to swallow it with Hants' steely eye still on him. "They're a kid? We're looking for some spotty, moody teenager!"

"We're looking for a juvenile who has broken the law," Hants replied matter-of-factly.

"Again – how do you propose to find them?"

"I have a suspect list of eighty-seven."

Woodward whistled through his teeth. "Rather you than me. So, how are you going to do it?"

"I have some ideas," was all Hants told him.

After that, DCI Woodward was reluctantly accommodating. His air suggested he had mentally washed his hands of the whole affair, which suited Hants perfectly. Apart from insisting that he be kept informed of any developments in the case that might affect his resources, and be asked before, rather than after, the use of his officers, Woodward was happy for Hants to carry on and leave him out of it.

Hants then went to the local library to figure out which approach would best suit his purposes for unearthing the deviant as quickly and quietly as possible. There was no point in creating a scene unnecessarily. The Division preferred unprocessed cases to remain unnoticed by the public, so a subtle approach was going to require some local research.

Hants could not resist returning to the recreation ground one more time before finishing for the day (which actually meant taking his work back with him to the B & B). There was a summer's evening glow over the park, which he viewed from the low wall at the West end. The shadows were lengthened across the tarmac and the air was sleepy from the day's heat. The halfpipe was swarming with Boarders, the roll of their wheels sounding out across the field. Hants walked slowly and casually along the rail, trying to see the graffiti from this morning. But he caught no sight of it, just an empty cloud where it had been rubbed clear. Although he knew it was entirely illogical, Hants felt as if his deviant had been scrubbed away too. It highlighted the urgency of finding this deviant as quickly as possible, in case they really did vanish.

*

"Hey!" Greg's broad smile appeared on her screen. He leaned forward, one arm hooked round his knees and the other on his lap, in a position that was so familiar, it made Clara's heart ache and she swallowed around the knot in her throat.

"Hi, Greg."

"How's it going?" he asked cheerfully, "Enjoying your ridiculously long break?"

"Of course."

"What have you been up to?"

She saw herself shrug in the small box in the corner of the screen. "Not much," she replied. She felt bad. It was not technically a lie, but she did not want to tell Greg about the skateboarding. Not like this, when he was so far away. "Hanging out with Carver."

"That isn't much," Greg agreed teasingly, "How is the little creep anyway? Still at war with Jena?"

"Jena's on holiday. Carver's fine. How are you? Back in the country at last?"

Greg laughed. "Yes. For now, anyway. It's good to be back – you can't beat home. I was worried my housemate might have rented my room out, it's been such a long stretch – but I'm back for a couple of months now."

"When are you going to come and visit?"

"Greg lowered his voice slightly. "When Sandy's gone and Mum and Dad are back." He gave her a mischievous smile. "How are you surviving? Been dragged along to any social groups yet?"

"No, not yet...," Clara hesitated. "She signed me up for netball."

Greg raised his eyebrows. "Netball? That's a sport isn't it?"

"Yes, Greg!" She knew what was coming.

"But you're crap at sport. Why would she want to inflict you on some poor netball team?"

"Thanks," Clara said, grinning all the same, "I don't recall your sporting aptitude being much better."

"I was captain of the chess team."

"I don't think that's a sport, Greg."

"Detail, details. So, what did you say?"

"About what?"

Greg sat back a little, partly drawing up one knee, and rolled his eyes. "Netball. You're not actually going are you?"

Clara hesitated again. Greg's eyes narrowed slightly as he waited for her answer, as if he expected her to surprise him.

"Sandy thinks I'm going." Clara said, hating how awful it sounded, "I let her think I'm going." She looked sadly pensive. "I actively pretend that I am going to netball," she admitted.

Greg allowed his jaw to drop open, and then grinned helplessly. "That's terrible," he said with a giggle, "I don't know why I'm smiling - I don't approve at all." He tried to look serious and failed with a shrug. "I knew you had it in you - to be a rebel. Though trust you to go and take it to an extreme. A normal person would have a tantrum about it, get grounded and that would be the end of it.

"What are you going to do? You should tell her." He looked thoughtful. "Maybe not that you haven't been going - but certainly that you don't want to go and won't be going."

"She's going to ground me."

"Perhaps. Probably. But you'll feel better about it."

Not if I break the grounding to go to skateboarding lessons, Clara thought.

"I don't want to spend my break grounded."

Greg looked thoughtful. "Well, it's no worse than spending it hanging out with Carver... besides, it's not that long 'til Mum and Dad come back, is it?"

I hope not, Clara thought with an internal sigh. She just shrugged.

"Anyway," Greg said, leaning forward again, "You'll do the right thing, I'm sure."

"Why do you say that?" Clara asked with mild surprise.

"Because you always do."

Clara looked at Greg's smiling, confident face on the screen and suddenly felt the enormity of what it would mean to lose his good opinion of her. He was her brother, so she knew he would always love her and he would always be there for her; but if he ever changed his opinion of her for the worse, it would be a terrible blow. She could not bear the thought of Greg despising her or feeling disappointed, or that she had betrayed him. If his view of her changed completely, there would be no going back. She would lose his comfortable, confident conversation and that honest, broad smile, which at the moment saw her only as the little sister he had watched grow up, shared secrets with, taught chess to, and made laugh. Soon he might look at her as a stranger, as if he had never really known her or what she was capable of: doing the *wrong* thing, on purpose.

Yet the truth was Clara had never felt more herself. She wanted Greg to know that there was more to her than even she had known, and there was more to the world than they had ever known. There was more to life, more existing, more world out there than they had ever been told.

Clara looked into those grey eyes, copies of her own, and felt the fear and yearning we only feel when we love someone absolutely, need them to know us completely, but dread losing them irretrievably. The fear won out, as it often does, and she just smiled.

"I'll try," she said. "I promise."

"Good. Let me know how it goes."

In the background, a beeping noise sounded behind Greg. "That's my dinner," Greg said, opening his eyes wide, "Better go, before it starts smoking."

"Okay."

"Speak soon, yeah?"

"Of course. Take care."

"You too!" He waved cheerily and then the screen went blank.

Clara felt the emptiness of the room crowd in on her. She took a deep breath. Tomorrow she would have to tell Sandy. She had promised to try and do the right thing, so that was what she would have to do, no matter what the consequences.

Chapter Eight

There were two ways to target a teenage deviant. The overall premise was quite simple: target the weak areas. And there were two weak areas in the teenage life: family and peers. How these two areas played out was different for each individual teenager, but the general principle was that one battled the other for influence. Teenagers seemed to live in a world of extremes. Either they were very close to their family or they were at war with them. Either they were embraced enthusiastically by their peers, or they were rejected.

It took Hants all night to decide which area to target. He knew little about his deviant as an individual. He did not know if they were popular or a social reject. He did not know if the deviant had parents who were intensely supportive or indifferent. He had to work partly on gut instinct and primarily on what he could make out about the community of Greylinghurst. Targeting the peer group was a tricky option. Since it was the summer break, there was not the usual pressure of a close school environment to apply. Besides, when it suited them, teenagers could be decidedly uninterested or loyal towards each other. Even if they thought there might be a 'deve' in their midst, they might choose to close ranks rather than assist an authoritative body, or give a collective shrug and mind their own business.

The other option was targeting the family. Adults worried more about being seen to be on the right side of the law, particularly in a small community where reputation and status were more closely scrutinised and everyone knew everyone else's business. For most people, family built or broke a reputation: children of teenage years in particular. Would parents give up their child if they suspected them of deviancy? Probably not, Hants reasoned, but it might spur a change in the adults' behaviour or habits that would indicate such a thought had crossed their mind. And when people changed their behaviour or habits suddenly, other people noticed. Would parents give up another's child if they thought it might 'save' their own from becoming corrupted? More likely.

Hants had known parents of deviants to take last minute holidays, cancel their social life, withdraw their child from normal activities in the outside world, and even move house - to contain and hide their secret, in the hope that, with time, it would go away. This was in fact, the worse thing to do. People noticed. Friends, schools, neighbours, colleagues: all would be alerted, and it wasn't the behaviour of the deviant in this case, but the family's which drew attention.

Hants reckoned that his deviant's parents probably did not even guess yet that their child was harbouring a deviancy, or perhaps they had noticed something was different but were choosing to ignore it or put it down to teenage growing pains. All they needed was a little trigger to get the thought started, and, if not in them, then a neighbour, friend or grandparent. A trigger might even give his deviant a nudge that would lead them to inadvertently expose themselves. Hants finally decided on this as the plan with the best chance of success. A little pressure targeted at the home life might spit out his deviant into his ready hands. And all he would have to do was watch and wait.

*

Sandy was in the lounge, painting her fingernails when Clara came downstairs in the morning. The patio door was open, letting in a gentle breeze which took the edge off the hot morning sun streaming through the glass. Sandy was perched on the edge of the sofa, looking unusually relaxed in a grey linen skirt which fell gracefully over her knees and a pink blouse with loose cap sleeves that lifted gently off her shoulders with the soft gusts that swooped at her back. Her hair was loosely clipped up, but a strand hung down behind her ear and against her neck, softening the line of her jaw as she bent forward and expertly applied the varnish. For a moment, her features were almost soft, but then she looked up and, seeing Clara, her stern lines returned.

"Yes?" she asked politely, but without any real invitation.

"May I talk to you about something?" Clara asked, trying to keep her voice steady but relaxed.

"What? I haven't got long – I'm going out in a minute." She slicked colour on to the last nail, replaced the cap on the varnish and blew across her fingertips.

"It's about netball," Clara said.

Her aunt did not say anything but rested her hands, palms down, on her knees and raised her eyebrows expectantly.

Clara swallowed and continued. "I'm not very good at it. In fact, I'm very bad at it and I really don't enjoy it. I'd rather not be in the netball club."

"You're telling me you don't want to go?" Sandy said calmly.

"Yes."

"There was the offer of another club –

hockey, lacrosse…" She left the options hanging for a moment.

Clara realised the expected response was to choose another sports club to join.

"Thank you for the offer," she said slowly. "But I'd rather not do something else – I'd rather just do what I normally do. Jena's coming back soon."

"A sport will be good for you. You'll be healthy, meet other girls your own age, keep occupied."

It was as if Clara had not said anything at all. Clara looked at her aunt, knowing that this was the moment she had to choose whether she backed down or saw her point through to the end.

"That's true," she agreed calmly, "But I hate team sports. I'm not inactive anyway – I'll go cycling every afternoon if you like, and Jena and I usually go swimming when she's around." She could see Sandy's eyes narrowing, but she was not deterred. "And I already know enough girls my age – to be honest, I don't have a lot in common with most of them and they're not always the good influence you think they'd be. I already have hobbies and friends that I want to spend my time with."

Now Sandy gave one of her ladylike snorts. "You mean that boy next door? I hardly think he's a suitable friend. He's hardly the sort of person you should be hanging around with. And as for girls," she continued, touching her nails lightly to see if they were dry, "Perhaps you should try having more in common with them."

Now Clara's voice took on the quietly assured tone it had when she had spoken to Rocket. "Carver is my neighbour. I like him and my parents like him. And they like me – the way I am. I like me the way I am. I'm not going to change."

Sandy got to her feet, her fingers twitching. It was clear she would ordinarily bunch her hands on her hips, but her fingernails were not quite dry.

"You will go where I send you and when I send you," she said, her voice sharp with controlled anger. "You will behave how I expect you to behave. And you will do as I say or you *will* regret it."

For a second they looked at each other and it was clear that neither was going to back down. There was nothing more that Clara could say to change her aunt's opinion, and all she could do now was convince Sandy that she meant what she had said.

"I'm not going to netball," Clara stated and turned and walked out of the room. She picked up her rucksack from the hall and opened the front door.

"Where are you going?" Sandy snapped,

following her as far as the threshold of the lounge. "You are grounded."

Clara glanced over her shoulder and gave her aunt a look that was almost sad. "I'm going out," she said, and closed the front door behind her, leaving Sandy staring at it as if she would draw her niece back with the sheer force of her will.

Clara walked up the road as quickly as she could and without looking back, despite the temptation. Guilt was pulling at her, wanting to drag her back to the house, beg forgiveness and submit to the consequences and the misery. She was a good girl, brought up to follow a certain code which she had just now betrayed. And for what? A week of skateboarding. A week of freedom. Possibly her last week of freedom.

If she had felt Sandy's demands were born out of a love and care for her as a person, she would probably have submitted. But Sandy had no affection for her. Clara felt as if she was a mistake in her aunt's eyes that needed rectifying, and Sandy's approach to that was twofold. On the one hand, she seemed to be erasing Clara from her life, cutting her out of the domestic routine, chasing her out of her presence with silences and a turn of that cold, straight back. And then, when Clara would not disappear, she tried the other approach of moulding her into her own ideas of right behaviour.

But Clara would not be moulded. She would not bend. She did not know how to. Clara was one of those people who did not have the art of pretence. She did not know how to put on a different smile or wear a different air or express herself in a way other than what came naturally. Her only means of pretending was to withdraw. She could hide what she was feeling and who she was, but she could not change it, even for appearance's sake or to fit in.

Clara tried to avoid replaying the confrontation in her head and focused on the gentle bump of the rucksack on her back. As she neared the recreation ground, it was like entering another world and she felt the guilt subside.

Unusually, Flinn was there before her, sitting on the flat of the halfpipe with his heels scuffing the tarmac.

"Are you all right?" was the first thing he asked her, looking mildly concerned.

"I'm grounded."

"You told your aunt."

"I said I wasn't going to netball."

"You didn't tell her about the skateboarding?"

"No."

Flinn grinned and stood up. "Well, who

would have thought a nice, middle-class village girl like you would turn out worse than a Boarder?"

"You've never been grounded?" Clara asked incredulously.

"Never."

"Not even after getting into a fight with Rocket's gang?"

"That was an one-off. And I got a long lecture on the dangers of fighting. A *long* lecture."

"That seems terribly unfair."

"Yep," Flinn agreed without sympathy, "Come on then, let's see if getting grounded was worth it. Are you going to be a natural at tricks or is the ollie the only one you'll ever master?"

After half an hour, Clara was inclined to think it would be the latter. No matter how she tried, she just could not master the pop shove-it. It felt like there were too many things to remember to do at once, and not enough time to do them before she hit the ground. It would be easier to learn if slow motion were possible, Clara thought; then she felt despair as she remembered this was one of the most basic tricks. She glanced across at Flinn, who was watching her patiently as usual, and realised that it did not actually matter. The skateboarding had become of secondary importance and it was the company she was really buying.

Flinn gave her a time-out sign and, leaving her board on the ground, Clara crawled onto the halfpipe and slumped with her back against the wall, staring at the blank streak in the graffiti opposite.

"I'm never going to get it," she said flatly as Flinn joined her.

"You will," Flinn replied. He said it with such confidence that it sounded more like a command. "You're thinking too much."

"About what?"

"About what you're doing."

"I've never been accused of that before," Clara said dryly.

"Sometimes, once you know the instructions, you have to forget about them and go with your instinct," Flinn explained, "It's as much about feeling how to do the trick as knowing how to do it."

"How long did it take you to get it?"

He held up a finger and thumb.

"Two hours?"

"Two attempts."

She shoved him gently on the shoulder and he shoved her back. Then they sat and stared ahead for a moment, baking on the hot surface of the concrete around them.

"We did graffiti in Art," Clara confessed suddenly, "It was one of our projects – to design something for an area in the school or community."

"Where did you pick?"

"Somewhere sensible - where the recycling bins are kept at school."

"Did they actually let you paint it?"

"No. They're not crazy."

"There's a skateboarding event next week, in Hampton."

Clara turned her head to look at Flinn. He had sounded a little awkward for a moment, as if he had been waiting to blurt the information out.

"It runs for three days," he continued, "We're planning on going."

"Who will pick up Rosie?"

Clara was merely wondering aloud. Flinn gave her a funny sideways glance. Little did she know that such a question did not have as simple an answer as you might expect. Flinn wondered if he should give her the complicated truth or simplify it with a half-truth. As he was still convinced she was keeping something from him, he opted for the latter.

"Our dad should be back then," he said, "He's in the marines."

"Did he teach you how to fight?"

"Yes." Flinn smiled, "You're not going to ask me to teach you that as well?"

"I can't afford it."

He just smiled and stared back at the wall. "Shiz - it's hot," he said, and then got to his feet.

Clara raised her eyebrows as she also stood up and they collected their boards. "Is that your version of swearing?"

"I try not to," Flinn responded with a grimace, "Or Rosie will pick it up." He gave her one of his smiles: "*Then* I'd be grounded."

*

Hants sat in his small B&B room and allowed himself to feel particularly satisfied with his day. He had set the little chair, provided with the room, in front of the low coffee table that the tea-making facilities had been set out on. These had been removed to the floor and in their place he had propped his Slate with a keyboard and phone beside it. Next to the phone was a neat stack of shiny leaflets, glossy and printed in colour. The top one read: 'Detecting Deviancy' in bold letters across the top and then beneath that: 'Protect your family – before it's too late'.

It wasn't perfect, but Hants was satisfied, especially as he had designed, proofread and printed them in less than twelve hours. On top of that, he had negotiated with

Woodward the appropriation of several officers (in plain clothes of course) so the leaflets could be delivered the next day. The last thing Hants wanted was even a suggestion of police presence. That would most likely scare his target audience into silence, or alert his deviant that they were being flushed out. It was quite common for local councils or charities to distribute such material every now and then, so that was the guise these leaflets were going out under.

Tomorrow the leaflets, his 'triggers', would be delivered; and then all Hants had to do was wait. He could have allowed himself the rest of the day off, but instead he sat in front of his Slate and reviewed the latest data in the Division's database. The only sign that he was not officially working was the tie that hung undone around his neck, and his rolled up shirt sleeves. This was practically a state of untidiness for Hants, who was never seen out of an immaculate suit.

Hants had no doubt that his plan would work. It might take a few days, but soon enough he would have something to lead him to his deviant. A little more patient waiting and watching and he would be removing yet another poisonous barb from society and handing them over to be dealt with by the rehabilitation camps.

It would be more flattering to say that Hants viewed deviants as numbers, or more precisely, colours to be processed: that their gender, age and social and economic background did not matter except in its relevance to locating them. White, green, amber or red – the person behind the labels didn't matter: as long as the colours changed in his favour.

However, the truth was quite the opposite. Hants had an acute sense of the individual. He could picture their little lives, teetering on the edge of the ordinary and the criminal, each trying to avoid detection, carrying out their day-to- day life pretending to be normal and yet feeling the difference deeply. Even now, Hants had a distinct awareness of this deviant, whiling away their time until the evening and feeling the relief of surviving another day. And yet, Hants felt no pity for his quarry or pleasure at their future agony. It was not personal. All he felt was the satisfaction of a job well done.

*

Flinn and skating, Rosie and jam sandwiches had temporarily pushed her worries aside for the day, but they came rushing back when she finally turned towards home. She knew she had a second encounter with Sandy awaiting her when she got back and she was dreading it. Fortunately, Carver ambushed her at the top of the road with his usual cheerful cynicism. He insisted in dragging her off to the barn so he could judge her progress on the skateboard.

"So, you told your aunt?" he said at one point, after watching her attempt a pop shove-it without success.

Clara realised he had probably heard the entire confrontation from his garden. She remembered that he had told her not long before that it would be all right in the end. She hoped he was correct, because now it seemed far from all right.

Eventually, she'd had to go home and face Sandy, who was waiting for her with a face of stone and a short but very clear speech: She was grounded until her parents returned. She was not to leave the house or garden without permission or supervision. She was not to talk to 'that boy next door' whom Sandy deemed to be the bad influence that had turned Clara into a disobedient, ungrateful child. She was banned from television and laptop privileges, and would be sent to her room at nine o'clock every night, with lights out at ten.

This was delivered in a matter-of-fact way that made it quite clear there was no room for negotiation, pleading or repentance. It made it easier for Clara to give her response with an air of polite apology but determination: She would go to her room at nine o'clock every night if her aunt wished, and have her light out by ten. She had no choice concerning the television and laptop ban, but she would not spend the next ten days inside the house and, short of chaining her to the wall, there was nothing Sandy could do to prevent her coming and going as she pleased. Carver was her neighbour and friend and she would continue to treat him as such.

Sandy was infuriated, but there was nothing more for her to threaten except that she would email Clara's parents and inform them of her behaviour. This hurt Clara, though she merely shrugged in response and went to her room. She hated the idea that her parents would be halfway across the world feeling disappointed in her. And she would not be able to give them her explanation as her laptop had been confiscated.

She heard her uncle come in later and a hurried discussion in the hall. From her uncle's mild tone it seemed he had little interest in the matter, or had received an abridged version of events. She found her dinner plated up for her in the kitchen, so she sat and ate on her own there, while listening to the faint clinks and voices of her aunt and uncle in the dining room. Afterwards, she trudged back up to her room and sat on the window seat, carefully copying out the printed sheets that Mr Summers had left her. She had thought of an idea while at the barn with Carver, and sensed that there was not much time left for her to put it into action.

At five to ten there was a sharp rap on the door which was the signal for lights out. Clara slipped her papers back into the cavity in the windowsill and then, changing quickly into her pyjamas, got into bed. There came a second rap on the door and, leaning over to her side table with a sigh, she flicked off the light.

Chapter Nine

The rich aroma of coffee filled the hall as Clara crept downstairs. She could hear the quiet sounds of breakfast being prepared in the kitchen until she passed the door. The sounds then paused, as if the occupant was listening for her movements. Clara went straight to the front door and let herself out. As she closed the garden gate behind her she saw the kitchen curtains twitch slightly. Without wasting another moment on her guilt, Clara turned and walked up the road.

She was a little earlier than usual and the village seemed unusually still. She passed a young woman talking on her phone and a man in a baseball cap who whistled cheerily as he delivered leaflets. The recreation ground was empty and for a moment Clara was alone. She left her rucksack on the tarmac and climbed the ladder to the top of the halfpipe.

The view was still just as clear as it had been when she had first stood on this spot. A light breeze stirred and Clara felt like a bird ready to leap upon the wind and be carried into the blue of the sky, over the green world.

“I don’t think you’re supposed to be up there,” Flinn interrupted, climbing up next to her with his skateboard in one hand.

"Have you seen the view?"

"Yes." He gave her a smile as he put down his board. "Not bad, is it?"

"That's an understatement."

He smiled again and tipped himself off the edge of the platform on his board. Clara watched him rush up the other side, turn, and then roll at a much faster rate back across the pipe. He reached her platform and slid expertly onto it.

"Going to teach me?"

"Learnt the pop shove-it?"

She grimaced and he pointed to the ladder. She obeyed and watched as he joined her on the playground.

"When do I get to go on the halfpipe?"

"When you're wearing a helmet and knee pads," he replied, "And elbow and wrist pads too."

Clara folded her arms and put her head on one side. "Do as I say, not as I do?"

"I don't want a split head on my watch," Flinn replied casually, standing on his board with both hands in his pockets.

"Didn't bother you the first time I rolled down that thing."

"Wasn't my watch."

"Charming. Do I get my lesson now?"

"You're early," Flinn said, glancing at his watch, "We've got half an hour 'til the lesson starts."

"You're early too," Clara said, crouching down to take the board from her rucksack. She glanced across at Flinn with a curious look. "Why are you early?" She put the board at her feet and turned round.

Her heart missed a beat.

Rocket and his gang had not even caused a tremor in her, but this sight did. Standing just a little way off, like a curious pack of wolves, was a group of boys wearing baggy jeans and hoodies, and holding skateboards in their hands. One of them, whom she recognised as Ash, was standing ahead of them just a few feet away from her. He was as intimidating now as he had been before, and the long bruise on his face only emphasised the impression.

Clara glanced back at Flinn who looked as cool and as collected as usual. She felt ambushed. Ash looked at her for a moment, with eyes that were taking in every detail: her jeans with a hole in one knee, Flinn's hoody which she was still wearing as disguise, and her fair hair tied up away from her face. His gaze flicked towards Flinn, who had stepped forward off his board and still had his hands in his pockets.

"You sneaky son-of-a-bitch," Ash said simply.

"Ash, this is Clara," Flinn said.

"Yeah, I remember." Ash looked back at

her, thoughtful but not hostile.

"Clara, this is Ash."

"Hi."

"After my halfpipe?" Ash asked lightly.

"It's not your halfpipe."

Ash grinned. "Do you use it?"

"Flinn won't let me."

"Not without a helmet," Ash agreed, "And some pads."

Clara saw Flinn smirk, out of the corner of her eye. Ash's gaze turned back to him.

"I knew you were trying to get girls into the group," he said, "First your sister and now..."

"At least he's got good taste," a voice said behind Ash. The group of Boarders had gradually crept forward to see the conversation play out. The speaker leant forward and offered his hand to Clara. "I'm Marty," he said, and gave her a wink as he shook her hand. "C'mon, Ash," he said amiably, "It's just one girl."

"She's not supposed to be here," another said suspiciously. "We've got a rep to keep."

"Don't mind Radley," Ash told Clara, "He finds girls intimidating."

"Piss off," Radley protested.

"Got anything you want to say?" Ash asked Clara.

She glanced over at Flinn. "You set me up," she accused.

"I like her," Ash said with a friendly sneer at Flinn.

As if this was their cue, the other Boarders swarmed past them towards the halfpipe and Ash came forward.

"Suits you better," he said to Clara, indicating the red hoody, "So, what can you do?"

"Not a lot."

"She can ollie," Flinn said, joining them, "And she's nearly got the pop shove-it. Balance is all right too."

"Thinking grinders next?"

"Yeah. Which is why we need somewhere decent to practise - without any bother," Flinn said, giving Clara a shrewd smile.

"Why didn't you warn me?" she asked.

"Didn't want to freak you out."

"Yeah," Ash added, "Because this hasn't done exactly that." He slapped Flinn on the arm hard enough to make him wince. "Could have warned *me* though."

Flinn shrugged. "I *wanted* to freak *you* out," he smirked.

"I think that's more the effect you had on Radley," Ash murmured, looking across at where Radley was watching them nervously from the safety of the halfpipe, "Anyway, we won't be long, and then you can get back to your master class." He went and joined the others on the pipe.

"What are they doing?" Clara asked Flinn as they followed behind and stood in the flat of the pipe at the back of the group.

"Filling in the gap."

There came the clack-clack of cans of paint and Clara was suddenly aware of the irony of the full circle she had completed in just a fortnight: standing here on the halfpipe, surrounded by Boarders and probably looking a lot like one of them. Jena would be furious.

"Want to have a go?" Marty asked, nudging her with an elbow.

"No," Clara replied rather forcefully, though Marty did not seem to notice. She hesitated and softened her tone. "Thanks for the offer – I'm fine."

Someone lightly squeezed past her, putting a hand on her hip as they went, and then she flinched as Marty put his hand on her shoulder and pushed her forward with him to the front of the crowd.

Already, a couple of the boys had worked quickly on the bare patch of wall.

"We like to take care of our property," Marty explained, and then added: "Aw, Tonner – what are you putting that for…?"

Some groans and sniggers spread round the Boarders at the 'D' and 'E' which had already been created.

"You know that's just encouraging them," someone muttered.

"Encouraging who?" Clara asked Marty.

"The deve who keeps vandalising the pipe."

Tonner gave the others a rude gesture and carried on with a 'V' and 'E'.

"I give it a day," Marty called out, "And you'll be scrubbing over it with remover again."

Tonner made a second gesture and no one bothered him again.

When he had finished, the artist stood back and admired his handiwork. He looked brightly around at the others and announced cheerfully: "If that deve paints on my work again, I *will* break all his fingers."

"Why his fingers?" Clara wondered aloud.

Marty mimed squeezing the nozzle of a can to her. Someone brushed against her left shoulder and pulled her hood over her head a little. She looked round to see Flinn next to her. He nodded silently to their right where she saw Sandy striding smartly past the rail, her disapproval of the Boarders obvious from the slight scrunch of her nose and lift of her chin. She walked straight past and disappeared round the corner of the park wall.

"Safety in numbers," Flinn said, low enough for only Clara to hear.

Clara could not say anything, her heart had leapt into her throat and refused to slide back into her chest.

"Right!" she heard Ash's voice call, "Come on, you lot! Let's clear off. We've got a competition to prepare for."

The Boarders shuffled slowly off the pipe in ones and twos, and sauntered, with no apparent hurry, across the park to the gate. Ash was last to leave the pipe.

"Adieu," he said, half-saluting Clara. "And good riddance," he shot at Flinn.

He jumped off the pipe and started walking across the tarmac to where Marty was blowing kisses at them from the gate. Before he had gone a few feet, Ash turned on his heel and addressed Clara.

"Don't let him walk home alone," he said seriously, "Or he'll get himself pounded." Ash grinned and then sprang to the gate where he gave Marty's arm a twist and pushed him out of the park. They heard an indistinct, 'What? I was blowing them at Flinn…' and then they disappeared out of earshot.

"I assume that was a reference to Rocket," Clara said to Flinn.

"Ash gets a bit maternal. Come on then."

He pulled her off the halfpipe and Clara reflected that she had probably never been so manhandled since Greg had left home.

"The pop shove-it or no jam sandwiches."

*

The usual post was on the mat. Carver flicked through it as he walked through the hall to the lounge: a couple of white envelopes that promised bills, a card addressed to Mrs Hurst, and the usual junk mail of one-off sale offers and incentives to change Internet providers. As one glossy leaflet caught his eye, he stopped suddenly on the threshold of the living room. He swore under his breath.

"Carver?" His mother's voice came to him with exaggerated disapproval. When she got no response, she left the sofa and found him still standing in the doorway, staring at the leaflet in his hand with a look that made her stomach jump.

"What is it?"

He looked up at her and handed over the glossy paper. She read the words mechanically: 'Detecting Deviancy: Protect your family before it's..." She stopped reading.

"...Too late," Carver finished for her.

This was not good. If they had a leaflet, then every house in the street had one, including next door.

"This is to do with that agent," Mrs Hurst

said quietly. "They think some deviant is out there."

"They think it's a student," Carver said dryly.

"How do you know?" Her large brown eyes were looking at him desperately.

"Because they wouldn't target you – parents – otherwise." Carver said with a shrug, "Why do you think they came to me?"

"You don't know anything, do you?" she asked carefully.

"No," came the firm reply. "I wouldn't get involved with all that. You think I want to go back there? Another rehab camp? Move again? New school, new friends?"

"No, I know, darling." She touched his arm gently, "I'm sorry." She took the rest of the post from him and added thoughtfully, "I don't think your dad needs to see this – he's got enough to think about without some silly leaflet disturbing him." Then, because he looked so tense still, she gave him a hug. "Don't worry about it. I'll put it in the bin – then we don't have to think about it anymore." And she went then and there, and did as she had promised.

But Carver was still thinking about it. He was thinking about everything he had lost two years ago, when he had been blackwashed: the price he had paid and that his parents had paid too. And he was thinking about Clara and what terrible timing it all was. It seemed that sometimes everything conspired to collide at the very moment you least wanted it to.

But it had to be all right in the end. It had to. He had to be proved right, even two years later. It must all work out in the end.

*

'Detecting Deviancy:
Protect you family before it's too late'

'Children aged 11 – 17 are one of the most vulnerable groups in society for being led astray by deviancy. At a time in their lives when they are beginning to form an independent view of the world, they are more exposed to radical and potentially harmful ideas – particularly those that may be dressed up as exciting and enticing alternatives to the protective code of the law.

'...It is perfectly natural for teenagers to entertain such ideas – to even experiment with personal beliefs about the world and how it works...

'...the danger is when certain ideas become entrenched and the next step offered is a step towards breaking the law...

'A Guide to Identifying Deviancy in Teens

Remember the ABC of identification: Attitude, Behaviour and Character

- *...creating and implementing own, seemingly arbitrary moral code – particularly if contrary to established social codes...*

- *... fearless attitude towards authority and disregard for sanctions or consequences...*

- *...lack of interest in normal social activities and interactions usually appropriate for age or gender...*

- *...disappearing regularly for long periods of time without stating where or who with...*

- *... submissive or compliant personality suddenly becomes confrontational and non-compliant...'*

Sandy finished her second skim-read of the leaflet, folded it again and looked pensively at the glossy cover, whilst she tapped her nails on the table top. She paused to sip her fruit tea and then scooping up the leaflet decisively, slipped it into her handbag.

Chapter Ten

"Where are you going?"

Clara stopped at the open front door and turned to see her aunt standing by the kitchen door with a cup of coffee in her hands.

"Just out."

"Where?" The question was calm and polite, but said with no friendliness.

"I'm just meeting some friends."

"That boy next door?" There was a hint of scorn under the calm tone.

Much worse, Clara thought, *if you only knew.*

"No," she admitted.

"You're not going to tell me where you're meeting these friends? I ought to know where you are, in case of an emergency."

That was true. For a moment, Clara weighed up the sensible suggestion with the possibility that soon she might not want to be found so easily. What would Sandy do if she told her where she was going? Something to stop her from being able to go to the park? Would she somehow drag the Boarders into their family conflict? Clara did not want to lie and she did not want to be difficult, but something warned her not to tell just yet.

"I'll be in the village," she said, "I've got

my phone on me."

Sandy just shrugged, but there was a look in her eye as she went back into the kitchen which made Clara wary.

That was not right. It was too easy, Clara reflected as she headed to the park. Her aunt was not the type to give up the fight so easily. Something was coming, something worse than the grounding and the email to her parents.

It was not just the conflict with Sandy that kept her on edge. It seemed the further things went on, the less time she had until she would be blackwashed. She could not explain why, but she could sense the hot breath of something on her heels that wanted to drag her out of this world which she had protectively woven for herself, to face a new world of exposure and uncertainty. It was no one's fault but her own. No one had forced her to take up skateboarding. She could have gone to netball, and endured it until her parents had come home. She would have done that, in the past, when there was just her good-girl fear keeping her comatose and safe.

Now another force in her had been awakened and there was a battle between the two which had yet to be resolved. This new life in her wanted to be expressed, but because that possibility was limited by the

Divinity Laws, it was pushing on other aspects of her life. It was trying to declare its presence through other means, and the result was her sneaking out to skateboard.

The truth was Clara wanted it out. She did not want to hide her secret anymore, and the only thing that kept her bottled up was what it would cost her. If she was caught for more than just the skateboarding, there would be worse things to face than Sandy's wrath. And that day would come soon. Her blackwashing was on the cards, she knew - as long as it was not just yet.

As long as she had just a little longer. Just a little longer.

Flinn was waiting for her by the halfpipe, leaning against its edge with his arms folded. He was looking thoughtfully at the ground some way off, and Clara felt a small tug in her chest when she thought how he would think of her, after he found out what she really was. Perhaps it would have been better not to have taken up the lessons, not to have met his sister. Although they were not technically friends, Clara reminded herself, and it was just a business deal, it was going to hurt to lose him.

Flinn looked up as she approached and gave her one of his smiles.

"You are going to learn the pop shove-it

today – even if it kills us both," he said.

"Well, it's been a nice life," Clara responded, getting out her board and warming up with a few ollies.

"Remember – no thinking," Flinn reminded her.

She got it on the third attempt. Then she was so frightened she might lose it, she had to repeat the trick five times in a row to convince herself she had really got it.

"Finally!" was all the praise she got from Flinn. "Now for board sliding."

He went back to the halfpipe and pulled out from the shadows what looked like a metal rail with three feet: one in the middle and one either end, so that it could stand free.

"Grind rail," he said, as he put it down in front of her. He flipped his board into his hands and turned it upside down. He tapped the metal plates to which the wheels were attached. "These are the trucks. Grinds are tricks that involve travelling on an object using the trucks rather than the wheels."

He put his board on the ground and skated slowly backwards a little distance.

"The board slide is a little different. It's a basic grind…," he explained, "But you don't technically use the trucks…"

And riding up to the grind rail, he did a ninety degree ollie, so that the board landed sideways on top of the rail, and slid forward along it with the middle of the deck cruising along the bar whilst he kept perfect balance with his feet on either side. At the end of the rail he landed neatly on the ground and slid to a halt.

"You've got good balance," he said, "So you should find this easy."

Clara folded her arms with a sceptical look, but did not get a chance to reply. She heard her name spoken from the direction of the field and there was a quality to it which was part question and part accusation.

She recognised the voice immediately and it had the effect of flipping her stomach upside down with panic. When she turned, she saw a slim, dark-haired figure in a denim skirt and halter-neck top, holding a pair of sunglasses in one hand, standing on the other side of the park rail, like a figure off a postcard.

"Hi Jena," Clara said, almost shyly.

"What are you doing?" came the stiff response. Jena's eyes shifted lightly from Clara to Flinn and narrowed with suspicion.

Clara left her board and clambered quickly onto the halfpipe. "Skateboarding," she replied, trying to sound casual, "How was your holiday?"

"Skateboarding?" Jena repeated, as if the word was new to her. "Skateboarding?" she said again, this time with incredulity.

"Yes." Clara heard Flinn climb up behind her. "This is Flinn," she added awkwardly.

Jena eyed him up and down with unconcealed disdain, and he returned her look coolly.

"What are you doing?" she asked Clara again, this time with a mix of exasperation and anger. "These hooligans bullied us out of the park. Are you crazy?"

Clara jumped down from the halfpipe and stood facing her friend with just the rail between them.

"Flinn just teaches me to skateboard," she said simply, "I'm not a Boarder - they're all right really. It's just skateboarding."

Jena's gaze seemed irresistibly drawn back to Flinn. "Why?" she exclaimed, "Why would you… is he your boyfriend?"

"No!" Clara stated in surprise, "Flinn's a friend."

"I'm your friend!" Jena said angrily, raising her voice a little. "How can you be friends with me and him? They made you get on that thing…" - she made a wild gesture at the halfpipe - "and you nearly broke your neck. How could you do this? How could you become one of them?"

"I haven't become one of anything," Clara replied, frustration giving an edge to her voice. "It's because you're my friend that I got on that thing in the first place."

"Don't make out like this is all my fault!" Jena interrupted, "Or would you now rather see your 'friends' give me a makeover with their spray cans?"

"What do you think I am, Jena?" Clara asked, trying to calm her own tone down a little. "It's just skateboarding - nothing else. I enjoy it," she shrugged helplessly.

"I can't believe this," Jena said bitterly. "I didn't expect you to change like this while I was away."

"I haven't changed," Clara said quietly, "I just skateboard now..."

And I'm grounded for the first time. And I've been lying to everyone. She had changed, just not in the way Jena thought.

"And you're not going to give it up, are you?" Jena challenged sullenly, "Let's face it - you're a Boarder now, Clara - have the decency to admit it." And she turned and began walking back across the field.

Clara could not let it end there. It was not fair. Skateboarding was not a crime. Having new friends was not a crime. If she'd had time to tell Jena herself, instead of her finding out like this, she might have reacted differently.

"Jena, wait..." She climbed over the rail and ran after her.

Jena spun round defiantly. "I don't

understand why," she said tersely, "Why skateboarding?" She gestured expressively towards the park. "If you had a huge crush on him, I'd get it. But why? Why are you hanging out with them?"

"I enjoy skateboarding," Clara repeated, wondering how she could possibly explain it more clearly.

"No, you don't. You can't. You're lying." Jena started walking away again. "You're lying to me."

"What do you want?" Clara asked, her frustration intensifying, "What do you want from me, Jena?"

"I want my friend," Jena snapped, stopping again and coming forward to confront her. "I want to eat ice cream and tell her about my holiday. I can't believe you would do this to me."

"I am your friend," Clara said simply.

"No, you're not," Jena returned coldly, "You're ... you're a..." She struggled to find a word that would convey all the disappointment and humiliation she was feeling in that second. "You're a liar and... a... deve!" she spat out.

Clara shrivelled inside. She had seen the word painted on the halfpipe every day; she had heard it used occasionally as a daring insult between her peers, and, although she knew that one day 'deviant' would be a label attached to her by the system, she had never had it directed personally or forcefully at her. The emotional intensity with which 'deve' was applied to her in that moment surprised and hurt her.

It was clear Jena immediately regretted her choice of words, but she was too wound up with her emotions to retract it. Instead, she just turned and walked away; and this time Clara did not follow after her. She could not. The word Jena had spat at her was like a slap in the face. And although she reasoned it had come in a moment of heightened anger and was not really meant in its true sense, it still made her take a breathless step back.

When Clara got back to the park, there was something different about her. Flinn had not heard the rest of the conversation, but he could tell from where he was standing that it had not gone well; and when Clara stepped over the rail, she looked as if she had been delivered a stunning blow. She was trying to hide it, but there was something pained in her eyes.

"I have to go," she said with an effort, packing the board into her rucksack.

There was something about the way she avoided his gaze that kept Flinn from asking what had passed between her and her friend.

"Sorry," she said apologetically, "Say 'hi' to Rosie." She tried a smile. "I've got to go."

Flinn resisted the urge to grab her and shake her and demand that she tell him what was *really* going on. Instead, he returned the smile and shrugged lightly. "All right," he agreed. "But don't think you're getting out of doing the board slide."

She made a face at him and quickly left.

Flinn was left on his own in the park, feeling helpless but without really knowing why.

Clara walked out of the village. She set out at a brisk pace, as if she was trying to escape a hound from hell, and did not let up until she reached the side track that led to the old barn. She had deliberately paid attention to its whereabouts on her second visit with Carver, with the express intention of coming back on her own. She had meant to come the day before, but the ambush by the Boarders had completely put it from her mind. Now, the confrontation with Jena had brought the necessity of her journey into sharp relief.

She clambered quickly over the stile and walked through the brittle grasses to the broken area of concrete. She put her rucksack down, opened the front pocket and took out a bundle wrapped in a plastic bag. Inside was the material Mr Summers had passed on to her. She had spent hours alone in her room copying them by hand, as he had instructed and now she needed to hide the originals. Clara knew that the first thing that would happen if she came under suspicion would be a search for such items. If they found her handwritten copies they would be destroyed, but this would not matter if the originals were safe. It was extremely difficult to get hold of documents like these, which were kept in a few basement archives under tight security. As historians, her parents had to get written permission to gain access to similar ancient documents, and they had described to her how the texts were chained to the shelves and watched by closed-circuit cameras, twenty-four hours a day. Getting copies of these texts had cost someone a lot of time and effort; they taken a big risk for the sake of others, so, as a beneficiary, Clara had to try to protect the material now.

Clara did not know why, but she felt that even if she never made it back to this field again, the fact that these papers were safely hidden would mean something to somebody at some future time.

She walked carefully across the concrete slabs, testing certain broken sections. Quite near to the shell of the barn, she found a slab that had loosened through the efforts of a large gorse bush, just enough to force her fingers under one edge and ease it up.

Beneath it, the earth was dry and crumbled under her hands as she dug a shallow hole under the concrete and pressed the packet into it, before lowering the slab on top.

Getting to her feet, she made a mental note of the location and then, wiping her hands on her jeans, collected her rucksack. For a moment, she stood on the baking ground and absorbed the silence, allowing her feelings to surface a little. She tried to work out how she could have prevented Jena's shock and how she might have handled the argument better. She had forgotten Jena was back from holiday. It had slipped her mind amongst all her preoccupations. She wished she could have told Jena herself about the skateboarding. Yet despite Jena's reaction, Clara was surprised to find she was relieved her friend now knew. Her guilt-wracked soul felt a little less heavy.

You've got to be stronger than this, she told herself in the quiet of the sun-filled field. You can't feel guilty forever. You're going to have to stand up for it all soon: who you are; what you've done; what you believe. Time to stop apologising. You made a choice and the real consequences are coming. And you can take it.

You will take it.

With that promise, she gave the hiding place one last look. And turning her back, with the feeling she would not see it again, she left the field, open and wild under the wheeling blue sky.

*

The trill ring of the doorbell sounded round the house and, with mild irritation, Sandy left her magazine to answer it. She was momentarily surprised to see a dark-haired girl, who looked older than her fifteen years, standing on the step. She had large, beautiful amber eyes, very fine features, and pearl-white skin. Only a small strip of red, dry skin on the bridge of her nose and at the base of her long throat suggested she had spent some time in the sun.

Sandy recognised her as Clara's friend; she had often seen them sitting together on the garden wall. Sandy's sharp suspicion made her immediately notice that the girl's full, pale lips were turned down sadly at the corners, and that her eyes kept flitting to the floor.

"Is Clara in, Mrs Michaels?" she asked politely.

"No," came the initially blunt reply, but then Sandy realised there might be an opportunity here. "It's Jena, isn't it?" she said in a gentler tone. "Is Clara expecting you?"

"No..." She sounded hesitant, embarrassed even.

"Would you like to come in and wait?"

Jena swallowed but did not answer.

Sandy looked concerned. "You don't know where Clara is," she said thoughtfully, "And I'm afraid I don't know where she is either..."

"I thought she might be at the park still," Jena said quietly, "But she wasn't there..."

"The park?" Sandy repeated. She gave the girl, who was now looking down at her fingernails, a thoughtful look. "I think you should come in," Sandy said gently. When she wanted to, she could exude an air of motherly care. "You look like you need a cold drink. The house is nice and cool – you can wait for Clara in the lounge."

Jena nodded silently and stepped cautiously over the threshold. Sandy made them both a cold drink and brought it into the lounge, where Jena was perched on the edge of the sofa as if unsure she was really allowed to be there.

"Thank you," she said politely, taking the drink.

Sandy waited for Jena to take a few sips and settle back on the sofa before she began her coaxing.

"You've been at the park with Clara this morning?" she asked nonchalantly.

"I saw her there," Jena replied, her frown deepening a little.

"Oh? She was with someone else?...Of course," Sandy added smoothly, "You've been on holiday, haven't you?"

"Yes. We got back late yesterday."

"I've been wondering where Clara's been disappearing off to this past week. She wouldn't tell me, for some reason." she dropped her voice to suggest a slightly saddened tone, "As long as she's safe I suppose." And she sighed and gazed over Jena's shoulder.

"I'm surprised she hasn't broken her neck yet," Jena muttered. She caught Sandy's surprised look. "I'm exaggerating, of course," she said hurriedly, "Though you could easily break something on that halfpipe..."

"Halfpipe?" Sandy echoed, trying to keep hold of her horror and, above all, anger.

"Clara's right," Jena said, her voice suddenly trembling, "It's all my fault really. If I had minded my own business in the first place...," she sniffed.

"It's all right," Sandy said soothingly, trying to keep up with this disjointed confession, "I'm sure it's not your fault. Clara makes her own decisions."

"Yes – but she only did it so they wouldn't attack me."

Sandy could not stop the alarm spreading on to her face this time. Jena realised suddenly how her exclamation must have sounded and hurried to correct any misunderstanding.

"Before I went away, we were in the park and the Boarders – the skateboarders – were graffitiing the halfpipe. I challenged them and they didn't like it much, so they threatened to give me a 'makeover' of their own – with their spray cans." Seeing Sandy nodding sympathetically, she continued, "They said if I didn't ride a skateboard down their stupid halfpipe, they'd carry out this threat. But I've got a bad knee – not that they believed me – I'd taken the bandage off because I didn't want to get any tan marks – I'm not allowed to do any sports for a while. Then they saw that Clara was with me and said if she did it – ride on the halfpipe – they'd leave me alone. So she did. Of course she fell off and hurt herself." Jena paused, twisting the end of her skirt nervously.

Sandy wondered how she had missed this. She ransacked her memory and, coming up blank, decided her niece must be a particularly deceptive child to have kept this from her. "Well," she said gently, realising her guest needed further prompting to continue, "It wasn't your fault – we should stand up and say something when we see someone doing something wrong. I'm glad Clara was there to support you – though I don't think you should take these boys too seriously."

"Oh, they meant what they said," Jena replied bitterly. "They're Boarders. They never deliver a threat without meaning it. I just can't believe Clara's become one of them."

Sandy nearly spat her drink back out. Instead, she raised her hand to her mouth and swallowed painfully.

"Pardon?" she said innocently.

"Carver was just joking," Jena continued miserably, "But I can't believe Clara decided to... skateboard." The last word came out angrily. "You don't expect people to change like that just because you've gone on holiday. I don't understand. I'm her friend – why would she want anything to do with them?"

There was a thoughtful silence whilst Jena tried to recover from her outburst. "I'm sorry," she murmured finally.

"So," Sandy managed to say calmly, "Clara's been skateboarding with these Boarders at the park every day?"

Jena nodded and sipped the rest of her drink miserably. She glanced about her uncomfortably as if suddenly unsure she should be there.

"And you saw her there this morning? And she hadn't told you she's been skateboarding?"

"I've been away."

"And... I suppose the boy next door – Carver? I suppose he was there too?"

"Carver?" Jena snorted dismissively, "No way!"

"But you don't know where she is now?"

"No..." The embarrassment returned and Jena quickly put down her drink. "We had an argument... we... I said some things..." She twisted her skirt and then stood up and smoothed it out. "I should get home."

Sandy stood up also, with a fond smile that was genuine this time; this girl had given her everything she needed to know, and so easily.

"Of course. Shall I tell Clara you stopped by?"

"No," Jena replied abruptly, "I'll... call her tomorrow."

Sandy showed her politely to the front door. Jena stopped on the step, an anxious look on her face.

"You... don't mind the skateboarding – do you?"

Sandy thought carefully before responding. "Not the skateboarding," she lied, "But from your description of these boys, I'm not sure Clara's in good company."

Jena looked reassured. "Thank you, Mrs Michaels."

As soon as Jena had gone, Sandy went straight to the study where she had left her handbag. She took out the leaflet and quickly opened it, scanning with hungry eyes. She smiled to herself with satisfaction. It all made sense now: the defiance, the lying and now the skateboarding. It added up to one thing: her niece needed help; she needed correcting and that was what she was here for. Sandy believed she was acting in Clara's best interest. It was clear Clara had allowed herself to be corrupted and now she needed saving; and she, her much-abused aunt, was going to save her.

There was a number on the back of the leaflet. She picked up the phone, dialled the number and admired her nails whilst it rang.

When Clara got home shortly afterwards, Sandy gave her no indication of what she knew. Having been instructed to 'carry on as usual' with the promise that someone would get back to her within twenty-four hours, this is exactly what she did.

Clara spent the rest of the day in her room and Sandy left her to it, plating up her dinner and leaving it in the kitchen again in the evening. She did not tell her husband what she had done, fearing he would disapprove out of misguided and rather naïve ideas concerning family loyalty. After all, being the brother of Clara's mother, his judgement would be clouded.

As usual, Sandy did not speak to Clara at all, and at five minutes to ten she tapped on her bedroom door to signal lights out. For a moment, she hesitated outside, wondering what was going on the other side. A minute later, the light under the door went out and Sandy descended the stairs, content in the belief that soon she would know anyway.

Chapter Eleven

Clara's heart jumped temporarily out of her body as the board touched the metal rail. The momentum carried it forward as she kept her feet lightly balanced on either end of the board and slid along as if she was travelling on air. As the end of the rail disappeared, she landed with bent knees and slid to a stop, feeling her heart drop back into her chest and start pumping overtime.

Flinn was right, the board slide was easier. That was her fifth attempt and she had done it: perhaps without much style, but she had done it.

"I am a good teacher," Flinn said simply, "Thank goodness that didn't take you a week..."

"The pop shove-it did not take me a week," Clara protested, pulling off her hoody, "It's so hot! How can you wear this all the time?"

"Again," Flinn said, nodding at the grind rail.

Clara did the board slide a couple more times, much more smoothly, and then demonstrated that she could still do the pop shove-it too.

"Good," Flinn said, "Want to try the board slide front-side?"

"What does that mean?"

"Backwards."

"No," Clara said decidedly, putting her hands in her pockets. Something crumpled under one palm and she squeezed it in puzzlement.

Flinn grinned and grabbed his board and the grind rail. "All right. But let's not have jam sandwiches today – I'm trying to persuade Rosie she wants peanut butter instead."

"Peanut butter and jam?" Clara teased, as she collected her rucksack.

She looked down at the crisp rectangular paper she had unexpectedly found in one pocket, to find two ten pound notes in her hand. She looked at them in puzzlement and then glanced briefly over her shoulder at Flinn. She remembered standing on the pipe a few days ago, surrounded by Boarders, and a light touch on her hip as someone had squeezed past. Clara smiled to herself, put the money back in her pocket and her skateboard in her bag.

"Why don't I buy us lunch?" she suggested casually, "We've got time, haven't we?"

"If it means I don't have to have a tussle with Rosie over the jam jar, then sure, we can buy lunch."

"My shout – I'm pretty sure I owe you a jar of jam or two."

"True. But you're going to regret it - I'm very hungry today..."

As they headed towards the gate, Clara instinctively looked back at the halfpipe and a strange sensation passed through her. Suddenly, without being able to explain how, she knew that she would never skate on that pipe. The feeling only lasted a few seconds, but it made her nervous. Today, everything seemed to have a last-time feel to it. She hoped she was just being paranoid, but something was telling her to make the most of this day.

*

The police station was a dingy little place, situated in a glass-fronted building that had once been modern and sleek but was now just tired and ugly. Inside, it was small and cramped, with the front desk preceded by a small area with room for only two chairs and a sickly pot plant. The walls were cluttered with screens displaying copious amounts of information in small font, and one of the screens with a loose wire flickered intermittently. Hants did not know how anyone could spend any significant length of time in such a depressing place. What bothered Hants the most was not so much the size and state of the building, but the lethargic atmosphere produced by the general inactivity of the place. Hants always worked quickly and he was immediately irritated by anyone less vigorous than him. This little obscure department was, in his view, unashamedly sluggish.

The desk clerk, a young man with a rather heavy brow, which made him appear permanently half asleep, gave Hants a blank stare before slowly recognising him.

"Uh, morning, sir," he mumbled.

"Have there been any reports?" Hants asked rather sharply. His impatience came from the fact that he had not heard anything for forty-eight hours when he would, by now, have expected at least a couple of call-ins.

"Reports, sir?"

"Yes. I haven't received any yet."

"Haven't you, sir?" the clerk asked innocently.

Hants noticed the clerk's hands tapping furiously at his keyboard as he spoke.

"They haven't reached you yet?"

He glanced up to find Hants looking at him with eyes that would crumble a mountain to dust if it blocked their view. The clerk swallowed and decided he could not get away with a cover up.

"I'll forward them to you directly," he said.

"Please don't waste any more of my time," Hants said curtly, "Just print off what you've got now."

In seconds, the clerk had the paper in Hants' hand. The Divinity Agent's gaze flickered over it, mentally sifting the information to find the one genuine report he needed. There had been half a dozen call-ins: a neighbour complaining about boys next door who played loud music and backfired their car in the middle of the night; an anonymous tip-off about an entire family which, from the account given, were the local mafia; a reclusive old man who never left his house except to light a bonfire every Monday. Hants mentally tossed these aside.

Then there was a father concerned about the habits of his daughter's boyfriend. It was not that one either, Hants thought, amused as always by the number of opportunists his campaign had produced.

The fifth one looked more promising, despite the appalling lack of detail or precision with which the information had been recorded.

"Did you take this call?" he asked the clerk, pointing it out with a pen.

The clerk screwed up his eyes at the paper and then said, with relief: "No, sir. I think that was Merrick."

Hants read it again, and a light of

satisfaction came into his eyes.

"Something useful, sir?" asked the clerk tentatively.

Hants glanced down to see he was being gazed at as if he had just grown horns and red eyes. "Yes," he replied simply, and went to find the nearest interview room.

He ignored the protests of an officer, and shut himself in, holding his phone in one hand. He dialled the number on the report which, to his further satisfaction, was a mobile number. Home numbers were always risky in this business.

"Good morning, madam," he said smartly, when the phone was answered, "This is Agent Hants. I'm calling in regard to the report you made yesterday. Apologies for the delay in getting back to you. I would just like to ask you a few questions....Thank you." Hants leant casually against the table. "Firstly, you say there has been a change of character – could you describe this change to me?"

He listened patiently for a minute and his lips parted slightly in the conception of a smile. "I see. Secondly, are you aware of any law having been broken? You understand I can only intervene if a crime has actually been committed?"

His smile grew slightly. "Well, there is a course of action we can take to establish if that is the case… It would require your cooperation…Very good. This is what I am going to do. An hour after she's gone to bed, I would like you to call this number. That will avoid alerting her to anything unusual taking place. It's important she believes everything is normal or she might panic and do something rash… Exactly, madam, I'm glad you understand the situation…

"After you call me, I will arrive with a team. We shall be very discreet, you have my word – no blue flashing lights, no marked vehicles. I will call you when we arrive and then you will need to let us in. From there, you can leave everything to us…" His lips parted further still. "Thank you for your cooperation, madam. Please be assured we have her best interest in mind. I will await your call this evening. Good day."

Hants stood for a moment with that half formed smile on his lips. He made quite a terrifying image in the mirrored wall opposite: a tiger in an impeccable suit; a hunter with an ageless, tranquil face.

He had his deviant. He knew who she was, where she lived and what she had done. The trap was laid; the mouse had already unwittingly touched the catch; he just had to watch the hammer come down.

*

Shivering against the cold night, Clara stood with her back to the wall, hands folded into the front pocket of Flinn's red hoody, a strand of fair hair curving out from under the hood. She stood there for a full five minutes, contemplating the dark of the park. Above her, the still stars watched expectantly.

Tentatively, Clara took one hand out of the front pocket and flicked on the torch she had brought with her. The playground apparatus sprung up on the edge of the beam, distorted by the night into eerie statues. The halfpipe loomed in the light like an open vice, waiting to close on any intruders and crush them whole. For a moment longer, Clara stood listening and watching, checking she was alone. Once satisfied, she dipped the torch and followed the beam to the pipe, a gentle clinking pursuing her as her rucksack bumped lightly against her back. She climbed nimbly onto the flat of the halfpipe and slipped the rucksack off, laying it carefully to one side. She stood for a moment, torch held downwards, tuning into the quiet of the park.

She did not know why she was here. Her instinct for self-preservation kept tugging at her to leave and go home. It did not feel safe tonight, and although her eyes and ears told her she was alone and there was nothing to fear, her skin tingled with the sense of another presence. The feeling she had encountered in the morning had left a disturbing impression on her and, if everything was about to unravel around her, she did not want just to disappear as if she had never existed. It was not much, but she wanted to leave something behind to say she had been here once.

Clara lifted the torch so that it lit the wall in front of her, where the word DEVE leered with the echo of Jena's voice. She could not get rid of the word, it was going to stick - but she could alter it for a little while. She bent down to unzip her rucksack and a stone skipped on the tarmac nearby. It was only a small sound, just a stone dislodged, but it might as well have been a gunshot. Clara grabbed the top of the rucksack, turned off the torch and leapt off the pipe towards the field.

Stones did not skip on their own.

She leapt over the rail, clanging the bag against it and catching one ankle, which made her hiss. Then she ran. It was pitch black on the field and the ground was uneven. There was nothing to run towards except the darkness, and she could only hope she would not run into a tree at the end of the field. She dared not turn the torch on again, for fear that it would pick her out in the open field; she hoped that the darkness would hide her from any pursuer.

Clara was only certain she was being pursued when she heard footsteps gaining on her. They were fast. They knew the ground as well as she did, and they were clearly determined. Clara's heart sank to her stomach. She knew who it was. It had to be. Of course it did.

Inevitably, an irregular piece of turf made her stumble, and, although she stopped herself from falling, a hand grabbed the back of her hoody and a foot niftily hooked round her ankle, pulling her feet from under her. The move caused her to twist so that she hit the ground on her back, grabbing for the tackler. They both swore together as they hit the grass.

Clara did not even have a chance to catch her breath before her wrists were clamped to the ground and a knee was planted on her stomach.

"If you struggle, I will break your ribs."

Clara lay perfectly still, not doubting for a moment that he meant it. One hand let go of her wrist but she did not move, even when the torch, which had fallen from her grasp as she landed, was grabbed, switched on and a circle of light illuminated the ground next to her. She flinched as the edge of the beam gave just enough light for her to see Flinn, and him to see her.

He swore again, but without surprise. "I knew it would be you," he said with a sneer that barely covered the bitter tone of disappointment.

Clara did not say anything. There was no point in protesting. He shook the wrist he was still holding; she was still clenching the rucksack, and the cans inside clattered together.

"This should be good," he said cynically, "Why?"

"Why do you think, Flinn?" Clara said, trying to grasp hold of her mixed emotions which were writhing and slipping away from her control.

"Why don't you just say?" he said flatly.

"Why don't you?" she replied defiantly. "It's your word. You've got it sprayed on your halfpipe. I am a deve. Satisfied? I am a deviant." It was the first time she had said it aloud, and it was like opening a flood gate. "Why are you surprised? Because you thought I was just some nice village girl? And why does it matter? I'm allowed to believe what I want."

"You lied," Flinn said simply.

"No, I didn't. I just obscured the truth," Clara said wryly, "What does everyone expect? It's not like I can say, 'By the way – this is what I believe', because it's against the law. Do you know what happens when someone like me is blackwashed?"

"You graffitied the halfpipe," Flinn said matter-of-factly. His voice was calm with the objectivity of a judge. "And then you pretended it wasn't you. Not just once. Several times."

Clara would have preferred his sarcasm or anger to that cool tone; at least it would mean he had not disconnected himself from her. His current attitude seemed to erase their friendship. In less than a few minutes, she had lost him. Clara could not explain to Flinn exactly why she had done what she had, and now he had made it clear he did not want to know. She wondered what he would do next. For a moment, his blue eyes considered her dispassionately, obviously wondering the same.

Suddenly, he took his knee off her stomach and released her wrist.

"Stay away," he said matter-of-factly, "From the park and from us."

And he got to his feet and left her lying in the dark.

Clara reached out and turned off the torch. She lay without moving for a while, looking into the night sky where the stars hung like silver tears, and rediscovering her breathing and beating heart. She wanted to cry, but the adrenaline was still coursing through her and her tears were locked up behind her eyes.

Come on, she told herself, get a grip. You can't lie here forever. You've got to get up and get home.

Slowly, she rolled onto her side and got up on her knees. She paused to put a hand on her stomach, where she could still feel the pressure of Flinn's knee. It was not bruised, but her muscles contracted with the memory. With a short sigh, she got to her feet, retrieving both the torch and her rucksack, and began a slow walk home.

*

"Was that the call?" the officer asked as Hants hung up the phone and started up the engine.

Hants did not bother with a reply. They were only parked a couple of roads away, and soon he pulled the car into the cul-de-sac and parked a few doors up from the target house. He motioned to the officer to remain in the car and closed the car door quietly behind him. As he walked down past a few houses, another two cars parked along the road and four plain-clothes police officers got out and followed him to the garden gate. Hants pushed it open and, as he walked up the path, the front door opened, casting a yellow light towards them. Hants did not stop on the step, but went straight into the house, holding up his badge with a nod of recognition to the woman in the hallway.

"Lead the way, Mrs Michaels," he said calmly.

He followed her up the stairs with two of the officers, whilst the other two stayed in the hall. Halfway up the stairs, a deep, man's voice asked: "What's going on?"

Hants threw a glance over his shoulder to see a middle-aged man, tall and broad-shouldered, in suit trousers and a shirt unbuttoned at the neck, standing in the doorway of the back room. Hants ignored him and heard one of the officers say in low tones: "If you could just wait in there please, sir."

Mrs Michaels stopped by one of the doors leading off the landing, and at Hants' nod, knocked sharply on the door, pushing it open at the same time.

"You need to get up...," she began, sidestepping into the room and switching on the light.

She stopped, and Hants stepped in behind her. His eye quickly scanned the scene. It was a neat room, spacious and clean with a cosy feel. There were a few personal touches here and there: a noticeboard with photos and postcards; a bookshelf with lots of books and a few files labelled with different subjects; the corner of a dark green skirt caught in the wardrobe doors; and pretty pale-coloured cushions on the window seat. The bed had been lain in; the covers were thrown back, the pillows pressed where a head had rested and a quilt was crumpled on the floor on one side. But the bed was now empty. The window was wide open, and, apart from in the wardrobe, there was nowhere to hide in the room.

Hants signalled to one of the officers to check the wardrobe as he crossed to the window himself in a few strides and looked out. To the left there was a trellis with a mature wisteria growing up it: easy enough for someone light on their feet and with good balance to descend.

"Anything missing?" Hants turned to Mrs Michaels, "Phone, wallet? House keys?"

The woman, who was standing still by the light switch, her face pale and sick-looking, responded with surprising speed. She moved to the side table and opened the drawers quickly.

"Wallet and phone are here," she said. "No house keys. I can't see anything else missing." She went to the chest of drawers and opened them too. "I can't see any clothes missing..."

Hants turned to the officer still lurking on

the landing. "Go and find somewhere outside where you can see the road without being seen – and send one of the others up."

"I don't know what's happened," Mrs Michaels said quietly, but with an icy edge to her voice, "Why would she leave?"

"I don't think she's left, Mrs Michaels," Hants said. He had not shown it, but he had been stunned to find his trap empty; and his first thought was that somehow his deviant had been alerted and made a timely escape. Having made a preliminary assessment, however, he was now confident this was not the case and his carefully made plan was merely a victim of coincidence.

"If she's left her wallet and phone, and there isn't anything else missing," Hants explained, "Then she's probably coming back. I don't think your niece has any idea of the situation."

"Where has she gone?" the woman said, almost angrily, "Where could the girl possibly go to at this time of night?"

Hants did not answer, but glanced about him again at the room. Taking a pair of gloves out of his pocket and pulling them on, he walked towards the bed and flung the covers off.

"Come on," he said curtly over his shoulder at the officers waiting behind him, "Evidence first."

He stripped the sheet off the mattress and then lifted it from the slats, running a hand over each edge, pushing and prodding along every side. If there was one thing he had to give deviants credit for, it was being crafty at hiding things. Fortunately, Hants was just as clever at finding hidden things, but he had known some very ingenious, if not desperate, methods in the past. One deviant a few years back had cut up an illegal document into numbered word by word pieces and hidden them around the house. Once Hants had discovered one of the fragments and formed an idea of what he had done, he and a team of ten men had literally taken the interior of the house apart until the house was no more than a shell and they had every single piece of the text bagged.

Evidence was important. Without it, it was difficult to prove a Divinity Law had been broken. And if there was no proof, the deviant went free.

"What about my niece?" Mrs Michaels asked.

"There's an officer watching the road outside," Hants replied simply, "If he sees anyone, he'll alert us. We'll turn out the lights and wait - she'll climb back in through the window of course..." He paused in what he was doing as something caught his eye through the slats of the bed. "What did you say your niece did, madam? What is she into...?"

"Hanging out with boys..."

"Boarders, wasn't it? Skateboarders?"

He dropped the mattress and, crouching down, reached under the bed. He drew out a skateboard and turned it over slowly. The half formed smile reappeared on his lips.

"I think I know where your niece might have gone, Mrs Michaels."

*

Clara paused on the corner of her road. Although part of her just wanted to crawl into bed and go to sleep, so she could forget the whole thing, another part of her did not want to go back. Going back meant going back to Sandy; it meant a grounding that she had no reason to break anymore; it meant long days of isolation and alienation from everyone in her life until her parents came home.

You'll just have to endure it, she told herself. Get on with it and see it through, it won't kill you. She took a slow breath and, feeling resigned to her fate, turned her eyes towards her house. Before she could walk on however, the door of a car down the road suddenly opened and a tall figure stepped out of the passenger's side. He stretched his back, as if he had been sitting cramped up for too long, and then, locking the car, he strolled straight to her front door. After a second, the door opened and he went inside.

Clara automatically pushed herself back against the garden wall she was standing by and frowned in puzzlement. What was someone doing at her house at this time of night? The car had not just arrived and, it seemed, the passenger had been waiting in the vehicle a while. And if he was the passenger, where was the driver? She stared hard down the length of the road, trying to see if she could discern anything else, but it was difficult to see much from this distance and angle. She thought for a moment and then decided she needed a different perspective. If she crossed the road, the curve of the road where her house stood should give her a better view. If she could not see anything unusual, she would go back, creep in the way she had left and hope no one had noticed her absence.

Without hesitation, Clara slid quickly across to the opposite pavement and squinted down towards her home. She could see the front of the house, with the curtains drawn and a light on in the window of the front door. This angle also gave her a slither of a view of her own bedroom window, where the purple of the wisteria was illuminated by a source of pale yellow light. Clara crept forward, with her knees bent and crouched behind a car. There was definitely a glimmer of light at the side of the house and it must be coming from her bedroom window. Someone was in her room. Why would anyone be in there at this time of night? Who was the man that had gone inside her house? Why had he been waiting outside?

There were too many unanswered questions. All of the answers Clara could think of were not very encouraging. She did not want any more surprises tonight; she did not want to be caught. She had always considered being blackwashed and arrested by the Divinity Division as inevitable, but now that she had possibly avoided that fate, she was not so ready to give herself up. So what if they knew about her? So what if they had the evidence and the witnesses to convict her? If they wanted her, she decided, they would have to find her first.

Clara crept away from her spying place with her heart fluttering in her mouth. Then, as soon as she was around the corner, she started walking swiftly back towards the recreation ground. She took a slightly longer route that was not likely to be used by a patrol. She did not actually have any ideas about what she was going to do. It was nearly midnight; it was cold already and only going to get colder, so there was a long night ahead to wait out. Taking a bit of a walk, as long as she was careful not to arouse suspicion, would not do her any harm, and the most natural route was towards the heart of the village again.

Her walk took her round the back of the promenade and the few shops that stood along it. It was the eeriest part of her journey as - between the blind back of the shops with their shuttered windows, and the small, cramped houses on the other side of the street - the narrow pavement was overshadowed by a large, unkempt hedge. Within the tangle of the hedge was a metal fence which, at some point, had been deemed too ugly a sight to endure, so, to improve the view, the hedge was planted in front of it. Over time, the shrub had greedily embraced the fence into its heart, making the pathway even narrower. The strip of pavement was not long, and there was a lamppost on the side nearest the shops, which cast a glare of lurid light on to the gap in the hedge where the pavement flattened to join the road. Even in daylight, this section of the road gave the impression of being cut off from the safety of the public eye. Still, it was only twenty paces long and the imagination made it more frightening than the reality.

Clara had almost reached the lamppost, the halfway mark, when a figure came out of the gap in the hedge and ran straight into her. At first, she thought it was an accident and that another pedestrian, crossing the road had not seen her in the dim light. But when the momentum of the collision carried her into a dead end alley lined with dustbins, between two of the shops, and another two shadows appeared off the street, she realised she had been ambushed.

The figure who had pushed into her tore her rucksack from her and then stepped to one side to allow the other two to join him, so that her exit was blocked. The lamp cast just enough light into the alley for her to recognise Rocket Shard as he stepped forward.

"Hello, girly," he said with a smile, "Thought it was you. Off to meet your boyfriend?"

Clara slowly let out a supressed sigh. She could not believe how this night was turning out. She did not respond to Rocket's teasing, but looked at him steadily and warily. She was not afraid, but she was suspicious of his intentions - they were not going to be friendly.

"Ah," Rocket continued, coming forward

with the patient air of someone who is in no hurry to complete his business. "Not got much to say this time?"

He reached within a foot of where she was standing before he stopped. And then his fist struck out, as if on a spring, and punched her straight in the diaphragm. The blow had the desired effect of knocking the breath out of her lungs. Clara automatically curled up round the injured spot, her mouth gasping silently and futilely for air. Rocket leaned forward and grabbing a fistful of her hair, pulled her ear towards his mouth.

"Try screaming now," he said in a low voice and gave a soft laugh as he took a step back, releasing his grip on her.

Clara finally caught a breath, just enough to half-fill her lungs, but it hurt as much as the blow she had taken. Glancing up, she saw the other two boys coming forward to join Rocket. Fixing her look on them, she bunched one hand against the tender part of her abdomen and slowly and painfully straightened up.

"I have a message for Flinn," Rocket said, "Which you're going to deliver." The casually-nasty attitude he had adopted suddenly dropped away and became far from casual. "It won't require you to say anything," he said, and slapped her face with the precision and power of a professional who knows exactly where to strike for maximum effect and with minimum effort.

Clara was unsure which hurt more: the blow across her cheek, or the force with which it made her neck snap round. Before she could fully register either, Rocket's hand clamped around her chin and squeezed his thumb and middle finger into the hinge of her jaw so that her mouth was forced open a little way.

"You shouldn't have crossed me," he said, bringing her face close to his.

Clara grasped for the vice holding her jaw with her free hand to stop herself being pulled off her feet.

"It's all right," he added, noticing her locked gaze on his face, "I've nearly finished with you."

He released her jaw, shook her hand off and struck her again with the back of his other hand, bunched into a fist. With brutal precision, he hit exactly the same spot he had struck before. Half expecting the blow, Clara recovered a little quicker, enough to lean her head back when the third strike followed it. She was not quite fast enough and took the hit on the side of her mouth. Immediately, she felt her lip start to swell and the metallic taste of blood on her tongue where her mouth had cut against her teeth. It could not have been a large cut, but it was enough to make the blood pool in her mouth, forcing her to either spit or swallow. Clara chose the latter rather than let Rocket have the satisfaction of knowing he had drawn blood. She sucked the side of her cheek and backed against the line of bins.

Rocket advanced coolly and grabbed her shoulder, pulling her towards him. He lifted his knee and she tried to shield her stomach by crouching down and folding her arms across her torso. But he grabbed her hard by both shoulders and pushed her against a bin. His knee smashed into her arm, knocking it aside, and followed with a second strike into her stomach. The impact did not wind her this time, but it did make her feel suddenly sick.

Slumped against the bin, she pressed her hands against the tender muscle and tried not to breathe. Rocket watched her ease herself to the ground, her face tightened against the pain. He cast his eyes over her with a look of professional satisfaction.

"Tell Flinn," he said, with a sneer: "Just a little taster." and with his two smirking friends, he turned and left.

*

The sound of the doorbell startled everyone in the house and drew Hants to the top of the stairs. He leaned over the bannister and listened as the officer was admitted. He was downstairs in an instant.

"What are you doing?" he asked sharply.

"I thought you might need me here, sir."

"I need you here like a bullet in the kneecap. You could have blown the entire operation."

"Sorry sir…" the officer stuttered, shocked and a little confused, "Have you not apprehended the suspect?"

Hants shot him daggers with his green eyes and returned upstairs without a response. The bedroom was being ransacked; one officer rifling through a pile of clothes on the floor by the wardrobe and the other inspecting every page of every item on the bookshelf. Mrs Michaels still stood by the door, watching it all with a determined gaze, as if she could will the evidence into being. Hants scanned the room critically, trying to imagine this was his room, his belongings: where would he hide something secret?

"Does your niece read much?" he asked.

"A little."

"Anything in particular – anything she seemed to be reading a lot?"

Mrs Michaels shrugged. "I don't notice

which books. The ones on the shelf I imagine – that or the letter."

"Letter?"

"From her parents."

"Where is the letter?" Hants mused to himself. He looked through the side table and chest of drawers again but found nothing. "Where does she do her reading?"

"In here."

"Whereabouts? Where does she sit?"

Mrs Michaels looked a little puzzled, but pointed to the window seat. Hants went straight to it and carefully took off the cushions, removing the cover from each one and expertly feeling inside. He knew that if a deviant was going to read illegal papers, they would often read them near a hiding place, in case they were unexpectedly interrupted.

Having discarded all the cushions, Hants started to run his hands over the seat, crouching down to examine every angle. It was while he was crouched at eye level with the window ledge that he noticed a seam in the sill. In less than a minute, he had opened the hidden cavity and taken out several documents. One set was a fat, dusty envelope addressed to the deviant in blue ink. A quick inspection confirmed this was the letter from the parents. The other was a pack of folded sheets. Opening these revealed neatly handwritten texts which Hants only had to glance at to know they were the evidence he was looking for. Finally, he had the proof for a conviction; now he just needed the deviant.

He looked over the papers again and frowned slightly before handing them over to be bagged up. Perfect evidence, but not the original documents from Summers' collection that he had been expecting. Those were either still to be found or had been destroyed, but they would not know for sure until they had the girl. He glanced at his watch. Still nothing from the officer in the street, but she had to be on her way home soon.

"All right," he said abruptly, "We've enough to go on for now – we'll continue the search when we've secured the girl. I suggest we wait for your niece to return now, Mrs Michaels," he said. "If she's not back in an hour, then we'll have to assume she's not coming back tonight."

Once he had sent everyone downstairs to wait in the lounge, Hants closed the bedroom door, turned off the light and settled down for what he hoped would be a short watch. So far, the night had not gone as he had planned. They had found the evidence, which meant they could now prosecute on the Divinity Law of

Communication, but they did not have their deviant yet. Hants had expected to have the girl charged and answering questions back at the station by now whilst the search of the room was completed by his team. As it was, he had a half-searched room, no deviant and plenty of unanswered questions.

As the time ticked on, he began to strongly suspect that his deviant was not coming back. Eventually, after an hour, he radioed through to the officer waiting outside in the dark somewhere.

"Anything?"

"No, sir."

"No movement at all?"

"Apart from Officer Cawley and someone crossing the top of the road, there's been nothing, sir."

"Someone crossed the road?"

"Just at the top, sir. They continued on - too dark to see any detail, it was just a figure, sir."

If he had believed he had one, Hants would have bet his soul that this figure was his deviant, but he could not afford to be sure yet.

"Did this figure appear before or after Cawley left the car?" he asked carefully.

"Just after."

"And you're sure they just crossed the road?"

"Looked that way from here, sir."

It was her. He knew it was. But there had been too many glitches tonight and he needed to be careful.

"Right, listen carefully! I want you to go next door. You won't have a problem - they've got a Red there. They've got a room opposite to here – I want you to watch this window for the rest of the night – I'll send another officer round. Understand? You need to watch this window."

"Yes, sir."

"You see any movement, you follow it up."

"Yes, sir."

Hants flicked the bedroom light on again and crossed to the window, which he shut and locked. It did not matter if she noticed it was closed; with the area under surveillance, she would not get far. Even if she did manage to escape, at least they would know that she was still in the village. Hants turned off the light as he left the room and went downstairs, where everyone was waiting in the lounge, looking dead-tired and a little depressed.

"Tape off the room and set watch outside the door – we'll finish the search in the morning," Hants told one of the officers, "Mr and Mrs Michaels, I don't think your niece is coming back tonight. I've got officers on watch, so, if she does turn up, she'll be apprehended. If she contacts you, try not to frighten her - find out where she is and call me immediately. I'll be round with a fresh team in a few hours' time."

"What are we supposed to do?" Mr Michaels asked, angrily.

"Go to bed, sir. Sleep if you can," Hants said simply.

"My niece is out there - who knows where, in what state - how am I supposed to sleep? What if something's happened to her?"

"I understand your concern," Hants replied calmly, "But you must remember your niece left of her own accord. It is most likely she is somewhere safe - with a friend perhaps. I'm sure she is more resourceful than you imagine, and there is nothing more we can do at present."

Hants delivered his instructions to the remaining officer and then signalled Cawley to follow him. They left the house and went back to the car, Hants getting into the driver's seat again.

"Right," he said curtly, "Radio through to the station and tell them to alert all the train and bus stations and taxi companies. Send them the girl's photo. I also want all the CCTV footage from every camera on the roads out of Greylinghurst, from 9p.m. this evening. If she's left the village, I want to know about it straight away."

"Yes, sir."

Hants drove to the high street and parked opposite the recreation ground. He left Cawley in the car and crossed over to the park with a torch in one hand. Pushing through the gate, he paused for a moment to swing the beam round the empty play area, and then made a beeline for the halfpipe. He stepped onto it and cast the torchlight on to the wall. The word DEVE stared out from the concrete, but it was alone and there was no sign of any suspicious graffiti anywhere else. Hants ground his teeth thoughtfully before swinging the beam over the field as far as it would reach. Nothing.

It did not make sense: if she had not come here, where had she gone?

Perhaps she had laid a false trail for them, leaving her phone and wallet in the room so that they would think she was coming back. It was possible she had another phone and wallet her aunt did not know about, and was now on a train to the capital where she would be lost in the shadows of the underground movement.

Hants reined his thoughts back in. She could not have known they were coming this evening. She had gone out; that was a coincidence. She had come back, but had seen Cawley go into the house. The figure at the top of the road could have been her. So now she was hiding, and they had to find her. They would find her. Hants just needed a larger trap, and one was being set immediately. There was nowhere for her to go without him knowing, and tomorrow they would begin a search of the village.

*

Clara did not know how long she sat trying to control her breathing. Once she had got used to the pain every breath drew, she eased herself on to her knees and slowly crawled to within reach of her rucksack, which had been chucked to one side. She hugged it and pulled herself up against the wall. She rested with her forehead pressed to the bricks and glanced down the alley at the line of bins. It was possible to squeeze between them and curl up in a little hollow behind, where she would not be observed from the street and where the lamplight did not reach. With a last effort, Clara shifted one of the bins a few inches to one side and squeezed through the gap. Then she dropped the rucksack to the ground and gently followed after it, sitting with her back to the end wall and pulling her hood over her head. Then folding her arms into the front pocket of the hoody and pressing them to her body, she watched for the dawn.

Chapter Twelve

The birth of the morning was signalled by the dawn chorus. It began in the hedge outside the alley with a single sparrow calling to the first staining of pale white light in the sky. He was answered by another feathered fellow on a rooftop. Their shrill conversation seemed to wake every bird in the block and soon the air was chirping with a cacophony of cries and whistles. The cloudless sky slowly opened pale and then faintly blue around its edges, and the lamp outside the alley went dark.

Clara took this as her time to move. She did not want to get caught in the bustle of the early morning traffic. She expected to be caught at some point, but she did not want it to be yet. Her limbs were stiff and sore, and she was tenderly aware of every part of her body that had met with Rocket's brutality. Her stomach was the worst as every movement she made caused the muscles to contract, sending a stabbing pain through her torso. She decided, last minute, to discard her rucksack in one of the bins. She no longer needed it and it would only make her more identifiable.

She paused at the end of the alleyway and gingerly touched the left side of her face, which felt like heavy meat along her cheekbone and around the corner of her mouth. She wondered how it looked and if it would draw much attention. Adjusting the hood over her head and keeping her eyes down, she crept on to the pavement and followed it round to the promenade. Once on the high street she crossed over the road and let herself into the park. There would not be anyone here for a while and she just wanted to be somewhere familiar whilst she figured out what to do.

Reaching the halfpipe, she slowly climbed onto the platform, wincing at the pull on her bruised muscles. With a tired, final effort, she pulled herself round so that her legs swung over the side and rested against the wall, and sat looking at the quiet view over the harbour.

She had been there a while when a voice addressed her from the ground: "You shouldn't be here." It made her heart flip over and jerked her out of her thoughts. She automatically moved for the quickest escape. Directly down was the nearest exit and she clumsily dropped herself down the wall and into the bowl of the pipe. The impact made her give a dry sob as it jarred her stomach, and it took the last remnant of adrenaline to straighten up quickly. She heard rapid steps ascending the halfpipe behind her and a hand grabbed her arm.

"Shit, Clara," Flinn said as he pulled her round. He snatched the hood back from her face before she could recoil. "Shit. Who did that?"

His eyes took notice of her other hand, still subconsciously pressed against her abdomen and ran back up to her face. He swore again. "It was Rocket, wasn't it?"

Clara tried to writhe her arm from his grasp but did not say anything, cautious of what was coming next. Flinn held on.

"What are you doing here?" he asked.

"I was just leaving," she insisted, wishing he would let go of her arm, "What are you doing here? You're always where you're not supposed to be. Please, Flinn." She stopped trying to free her arm, too tired to fight anything now. "Let me go. I promise you won't see me again."

"What do you think I'm doing here?" he said simply, "*You're* the one always where you shouldn't be – I was counting on finding you here." His voice became gentler as he examined her face. "You haven't been home have you?"

"I can't go home," Clara said, her voice tight in her throat, "I think I'm blackwashed." her voice dropped to a hoarse whisper, "I've got to go."

Flinn released his grip on her arm and took her hand instead, gently pulling her towards the field. "Come on," he said, "Let's get you somewhere safe."

Flinn did not take her to his house; instead they knocked on the door of a house in one of the older quarters of the village, where most places looked like they were fast losing a battle with the shrubbery in their front gardens. The front door rattled as someone pounded down the stairs, cursing softly.

"Do you know what time it is?" Ash demanded on opening the door.

"Yes," Flinn replied casually.

Ash looked at Clara who was examining the ground, then at her hand held in Flinn's, and then up at his friend again. "What's up?" he asked gravely.

"Need a favour," Flinn said, and Ash knew that if Flinn was asking, it must be something serious. Flinn rarely asked for anything and Ash would never turn him down when he did.

"Sure," he said, "Come in."

Flinn hesitated on the doorstep and glanced at Clara. "Is Sye in?"

Ash snorted. "He's sleeping off a hangover so huge I'll be astonished if he wakes up before Chrissmass."

He led them into a large, old-fashioned lounge with an enormous, deep-seated sofa, a sturdy oak coffee table, wood flooring and a dining table against one wall which was covered in wires and electrical items.

"Got some ice?" Flinn asked, sitting Clara on one end of the sofa and perching on the coffee table in front of her. He pushed her hood back and Ash, standing behind him, gave a low whistle. He went straight through to the kitchen and came back a moment later with a tea towel bunched around a fistful of ice cubes.

Clara winced as she held it to her face and wished there was something that would ease the pain in her abdomen.

"What happened?" Ash asked, perching next to Flinn on the table. Clara felt a little like she was either being interviewed or discussed like an exhibit.

"You mean 'who' happened?" Flinn said dryly.

Ash swore. "I'm going to kill that little…"

"It's my fault," Flinn interrupted. He did not take his eyes off Clara. "What did Rocket say?"

Clara grimaced. "Nothing."

"It doesn't matter," Flinn said wryly, "I can see what the message is."

"So what's going on?" Ash asked, "You don't knock on my door at this sort of hour unless there's something else. There had better be something else," he added seriously, "It's not like you don't have ice at your house."

Clara looked at Flinn and realised he wanted her to tell Ash. He obviously thought Ash could help in some way, otherwise they would not be here; but they would have to tell him the truth because Ash was the sort who knew when he was being spun a story.

"I need to hide Clara for a bit," Flinn said slowly.

"You don't have to," Clara cut in quickly, "I wouldn't expect anyone to."

"Who are you hiding from?" Ash asked, raising an eyebrow.

"The Divinity Division," Flinn answered frankly.

His honesty and matter-of-fact tone surprised even Clara. They both looked at Ash, waiting for his response. For a moment, he just stared placidly at her, eyes scrutinising her pale face. He squinted slightly and drew in a deep breath.

"You're the deve?"

"Yes."

He glanced sideways at Flinn. "You know," he said, "You're lucky I like you and I like her…"

"I knew your maternal instinct would win out…," Flinn sneered lightly.

"Yeah, well," Ash returned, standing up, "Don't think my maternal instinct won't give you a good hiding if you get me nicked. I'm going to make breakfast and then we need to figure this out." and he slipped into the kitchen.

"Flinn...," Clara said quietly.

"You were right," Flinn said swiftly, stopping her with a hand on her knee. He took it away quickly and shrugged. "I don't blame you for not telling me – I would have done the same."

"I'm sorry for the graffiti," she said.

"So am I," he agreed. And she knew he was not necessarily talking about hers.

"Why were you in the park last night?" Clara asked hesitantly, not really wanting to call up the memory which was rawer than the bruises on her face. But she needed to know. She needed to know what he now thought, and the only way to find out was to talk about 'it'.

"I've been waiting for the past few nights – since we cleared the last lot of graffiti," Flinn admitted, "I figured... you... would be back."

"You said you knew it was me."

"It had crossed my mind. I didn't know for sure – I pretty much dismissed the idea, but it was in the back of my mind." He paused, his blue eyes fixed on her as if she were a book he was reading a second time after discovering his original interpretation was way off mark. She wondered what his conclusion would be this time. "When did you run into Rocket?" he asked.

Clara realised this had been bothering him since he had found her.

"After I realised I couldn't go home," she replied, taking the ice from her face and meeting his gaze, "Rocket was just bad luck. He's done what he's done and it's over. This...," and she touched her lip to see if the swelling had subsided at all, "Is the least of my worries. I've screwed up, Flinn. I've lost everything and it's no one's fault but my own. Do you know what it means when they catch me?" her lip curled in disgust. "I'll have this label attached to me for the rest of my life. Deviant. I hate that word."

"Don't you have your own word?" Flinn asked, "What do you call yourselves?"

Clara shrugged and then smiled slightly, a flicker of light warming those grey eyes.

"Mr Summers told me we were Divine Deviants - Diviners was the word he used."

"You knew about Mr Summers?"

"We spoke once about... it - and then after that he just..." She hesitated, but then it did not really matter anymore; they would have found her texts by now: "He used to leave me things to read - at a secret location. That's what they'll charge me with when they catch me."

"They're not going to catch you," Flinn said.

"I have nowhere to go."

"You'll be safe here until we figure something out."

"I've been thinking about that," Ash said, coming in with three mugs of tea and handing them out. "I reckon if we get you out of Greylinghurst, they'll have more trouble finding you. You should come with us to Hampton – to the skateboarding event. You can travel as one of us – stick some boy's clothes on you, hide your hair – they'll just think you're another Boarder. In a way..." He scrunched up his face as if he could not believe what he was about to say. "Rocket did you a favour – everyone's going to see those shiners and think 'typical boy, been in a fight'. People always see what they expect to see."

"I don't want to drag you into this...," Clara began.

"Too late for that," Ash said firmly, "I don't know which Divinity Laws you've broken, but you seem pretty all right to me. You're one of us now."

Clara swallowed and put the ice back to her face, as if she could freeze the tears which had started, unbidden and unwanted, behind her eyes. Flinn seemed to sense her reaction and stood up quickly.

"Come on, Ash. I'm starving," he complained, pushing him towards the kitchen, "I can't plan anything when my stomach is growling at me..."

Clara watched them disappear into the kitchen and then, putting down her mug, brushed the tears off her cheeks with her sleeve. Right now, she was in the middle of a catastrophe and utterly unable to help herself, yet it did not matter. She was not alone. And even if she did get caught, no one could take away this short moment when she was more a friend than a deviant.

*

Carver was fizzing quietly with impatience. He had spent a sleepless night lying on the sofa whilst two plain-clothed police officers commandeered his room. He had watched them set up at the window and then gone downstairs in the dark and listened to his parents' whispered conversation in the kitchen. Finally, they had gone back to bed, but Carver had laid awake, remembering and wondering.

So, he had been right: it was Clara; and now she had been found out, but not caught. She obviously had not been home when the Divinity Division turned up, so she would either walk straight into the trap or she had made a narrow escape. Carver held on to the latter hope all through the night and was rewarded in the morning when the officers upstairs were called off and the agent arrived a few hours later; he knew then that they still had not found her, or they would not be bothering with him. Carver had several ideas about where Clara might be, and he desperately wanted to find her and know if she was okay. The only thing stopping him at the moment was the interrogation he was being given by the Divinity Agent

"I imagine you are aware of the situation we're handling at the moment," Hants began, fixing his eyes on Carver and not shifting his gaze during the entire interview.

Carver did not say anything but kept his arms folded and his face as blank as possible.

"You were aware that your neighbour, Clara Slade, had joined a group of Boarders?"

It was not really a question, so Carver shrugged and replied simply: "She was skateboarding, but I didn't know she had actually joined them. Boarders don't usually take on girls."

"You were friends with Clara?"

Carver was amused by the use of the past tense, but he did not show it. He was not going to show anything to Hants if he could help it.

"We're neighbours," he said vaguely. "We hung out when Jena wasn't around."

"You weren't surprised when she started the skateboarding?"

Carver noticed he did not follow up the mention of Jena's name, which meant he knew about her already. He shrugged again. "It's none of my business."

"It didn't seem odd?"

"It's not illegal."

"Did she talk to you about the Boarders?"

"Not really."

"What did you do when you hung out together?"

"Walked round the village - talked."

"But not about Boarders or skateboarding?"

"We didn't talk about that stuff."

"So you don't know anything about these Boarders your friend was hanging out with?"

Carver gestured helplessly. "I'm not a Boarder. I stay away from them, like I stay away from Rocket Shard."

"Rocket Shard?"

"You don't get in Rocket's way – not if you like your face the way it is."

"Any ideas where Clara would go? Or who she would go to?"

"I dunno. Jena?"

Hants looked at him for ten seconds longer and then moved to the door. "If you have any contact from her – you'll inform us."

" 'Course," Carver said heavily.

He waited until the agent had driven away and then pulled on his trainers.

"Just going up the shop!" he called up the stairs, and then left the house, trying to look as casual as possible. He even paused to stare at the officer posted outside next door, so that no one would think he was sneaking off.

The Divinity Division obviously thought the Boarders would lead to Clara's whereabouts, and it would not be long before they got some names from Jena. Carver had to get to Clara first. He could not let her be caught without telling her what he knew.

He decided to try Ash Morgan's house; that might at least lead him to Flinn. Everyone knew where the Morgans lived, because the rivalry between Rocket and Ash was only exceeded by the hatred between Royce Shard and Sye Morgan. A year ago, Royce had thrown a brick through the Morgans' front window, and it had started a fight that required the attendance of ten policemen and three ambulances. Both were under suspended sentences and, although the main parties had kept their heads down ever since, the incident had stuck in Carver's mind. Knowing who might cause trouble and how to avoid them became an instinct after you had been through trouble yourself.

When Flinn answered the door, Carver knew he had found Clara.

"I need to speak to her," was the first thing that came out his mouth.

"You've got the wrong house," Flinn replied. His attitude was so cool that Carver was almost convinced he had.

Without thinking, Carver put his hand on the door and one foot on the threshold. Flinn raised an eyebrow and looked at him curiously.

"I know she's here. Please – will you tell her it's Carver. I need to speak to her. I'm not going to give her away, I promise."

"And if she was here," Flinn asked cautiously, "She should believe you because...?"

"Because I'm the other one," Carver said, hoping he had got this right. "I'm the other deviant. The first lot of graffiti on the halfpipe – that was me."

Carver was not even sure if Flinn knew about Clara or if he would be hiding her if he did, but he was not going to know unless he risked something. He braced himself for a painful reaction, a verbal attack or a physical one, but he got neither. Instead, Flinn just opened the door wider for him to come in. Carver was not sure if he was walking into an ambush, but he stepped inside anyway and stood awkwardly in the hall as Flinn closed the door.

Ash emerged from a doorway to the left and looked Carver up and down casually.

"If you're not a friend," he said casually, "I'll break your teeth. Come on – she's in here." He turned and indicated for Carver to follow.

Clara was sitting on the sofa in the lounge, but she started to get up when she saw him.

"Carver!" she said with nervous surprise, "What are you doing here?"

"What happened to you?" Carver exclaimed, putting both hands on her shoulders. He swore softly, but then unexpectedly put his arms round her and hugged her. It was only a brief gesture, but it conveyed more than anything he could have said and, suddenly, Clara felt more vulnerable than she had done so far. His pensive look, as they sat down, scared her.

"What are you doing here?" she asked again.

"I had to see you. There're things I have to tell you – before they get to you - you can't let them find you," he corrected. "You have to do everything you can not to get caught."

"That's the plan," Ash said.

"I don't have anywhere to go," Clara told him. "I don't want to drag everyone into this..."

"It doesn't matter," Carver said firmly. "Do you know what they'll do to you, Clara? When they've caught you? They'll send you to a rehab camp - and do you know what they do there?"

"How do you?" Ash asked suspiciously.

"Because I'm a Red," Carver replied, "An 'ex-deviant' - as far as they're concerned, anyway."

"You're a deviant!" Clara said with genuine relief. "It was your graffiti?"

"The first lot - yes."

"Two deves in my house," Ash said wryly, "Who would have thought it?"

"What happens in rehab camp?" Flinn asked curiously.

"They break you down - bit by bit," Carver said. "I know that sounds overly dramatic, but that's exactly what they do. They break you down: physically, mentally - in any way they can. Everything you've ever thought or known or believed they push to the wire. They press you, until you think you must be either evil or insane, or both." Carver's voice was tight with the bitterness of experience. "They rip it all out and then they stuff you with fear and disillusionment

– mostly fear. It's a lie when they say you're free to believe what you like. They don't just want to correct your behaviour or ensure you follow their Divinity Laws. Don't believe that they'll let you out if you still have the spark – they want to kill it."

"You got out," Ash said. "Don't you have the… spark… still?"

"I scraped out," Carver said with a hint of anger, but also shame in his voice. "By the time they'd finished with me I was so afraid – mostly of myself." He turned to Clara. "You have to do everything you can not to get caught." He hesitated: "But if you do get caught…"

"She won't if we can help it," Ash cut in.

"But if you do; if it comes to the worst case scenario and they catch you…," Carver continued gravely, "You need to remember this: there's one thing they won't do and one thing they can't. They won't kill you. It's not what they want - that would make you some sort of martyr and they don't want that. And they can't kill it – the spark, the divine." Carver's eyes met Clara's, and he laid three fingers on his chest. "That life, the eternal, in you – it can't die and they can't take it from you."

As Carver spoke, both Ash and Flinn felt as if they were eavesdropping on a secret they were not allowed to share. Flinn felt the tingle of goosebumps on his skin and Ash shifted uneasily, suddenly looking around as if for another presence. There was silence in the room for a full minute after Carver had finished speaking.

Suddenly Ash drew in a deep breath. "Well, I think I just heard some more Divinity Laws breaking…," he said jokily.

"I assume we can expect the police here soon," Flinn said practically.

"I reckon they've gone to Jena's," Carver told him. "They didn't have your names."

"They will have soon; she knows my name," Flinn said calmly. "And yours," he added, glancing at Ash.

"Then they'll be here at some point today," Ash agreed. "That's fine, we can deal with that." He looked at Carver: "Though you had better not be here when they come."

"Yes," Carver nodded. "Whatever you do, though, don't underestimate the Double D. They'll have everything covered – the stations, buses. They'll have a photo circulated. You'll have to be smart." He looked at Clara. "If you can get to the capital you might have a chance of disappearing. There's an underground movement there called The Assembly – I don't know how you find them, but it's worth a shot." He glanced at his watch and stood up. "Promise you'll try and get away."

"I promise."

He headed to the door and glanced over his shoulder one last time with one of his typically cynical looks.

"I hope I don't see you again," he grinned. "Not here anyway."

"Thanks, Carver," Clara replied softly, "Take care of yourself."

He gave her a nod and then Ash showed him out.

Flinn perched on the arm of the sofa and looked quietly at Clara as she subconsciously rubbed her stomach and gazed at the window. She was still the same Clara he had always known. Knowing she was a deviant did not radically alter the way he perceived her; it just made more sense of her. She was still the same reserved, slightly awkward, calm mannered village-girl, who was still holding part of herself back from him; he just knew what that part was now. The spark of a hidden life, which he had only glimpsed before, was now clearly apparent; but he still did not really understand it. He was not sure if he wanted to. Listening to Carver talk, he could see there was something Carver shared with Clara. Part of him wanted to understand what Carver had meant about the divine, the eternal life, but another part of him felt more strongly that he did not want to understand.

Knowing Clara believed in something - the divine, a deity, whatever it was - that was one thing. Understanding exactly what it was would be an entirely different challenge. Flinn was scared to understand. If she believed in a deity with nine heads that carried the world in its one eye, then he did not want to know. That would change his view of her; and he did not want to think that she was crazy or deluded. He wanted to keep her as he saw her now. Right now, he was happier in his ignorance.

"Right," Ash said, coming back into the room, "I reckon if the Double D are coming here they'll want to speak to you, Flinn. But they're also going to want to check out the house if they can."

"What should I do?" Clara asked, "Is there a way out the back?"

"Yes...," Ash said slowly. "But we have to assume they'll have that covered – they might have the entire street covered in fact. I think we keep you here, in full view. Give you a beanie hat, something boyish to do, and I think we might pass you off as another Boarder."

"That's a big risk," Flinn said.

"Yes, but if we can't pull it off here, we'll never get her out of Greylinghurst. If they think they've covered here and we're clean, then there's a better chance of us leaving without drawing too much attention."

Clara looked at them both and shrugged. "Okay," she said, "It's worth a try."

"More than that," Ash said, moving suddenly to the window, "It's too late to try anything else."

*

Hants stood behind the uniformed officer and waited for his knock to be answered. He found that, a uniformed policeman had a greater impact on civilians in these cases, and helped loosen their tongues. In addition, he did not yet want the public knowing that they were pursuing a deviant. The Divinity Division hated publicity in on-going cases. It did not want to give credence to a deviant by providing an audience to their deviancy. Once they were arrested there would be a news report, but by then there would be nothing to say other than that they were guilty of their crimes and had been sentenced. For now, the story was that they were looking for the girl because they needed her help in an inquiry and were concerned for her welfare. It had worked beautifully on the friend who had given them first names of several Boarders without hesitation. They had tried one already, but no one had been home, so here they were, at the next address.

The door was opened by a boy with mouse coloured hair and a yellowing, long bruise down one side of his face. He did not look surprised to see them, just suspicious, which was explained by his first remark.

"Are you here for my brother?"

"Are you Ashley Morgan?" the uniformed officer asked.

"Yes."

"May we come in?"

"That depends," he said simply. Clearly he was used to the police and Hants could tell this was someone who was smart from experience. "Who do you want to speak to?"

"You," Hants said, stepping forward, "And Flinn Raize. Is he here?"

"You're not after Sye?" He seemed relieved and then curious. "What's going on?"

"May we come in?" the officer repeated.

This time he shrugged, "Sure," and let them in. "This way." He led them into the lounge and the officer wandered towards the kitchen. Ash watched him with cold resignation.

"Is Flinn Raize here?" Hants asked.

"Yeah," came the bemused reply, "He's in there." He indicated towards a small back room, where low sounds of a television or computer could be heard. "Flinn!" he called, as the officer wandered back from the kitchen with a shake of his head at Hants.

There was no response for a moment.

"Flinn!"

"What?" came the slightly irritated reply.

Hants nodded to the officer who went to the door and pushed it open slightly. There were two figures in hoodies sitting in front of a screen, playing some sort of shoot-'em-up game.

"Flinn Raize?" the officer asked. One of them looked round, saw the uniform and gave a wry look. He pulled his gaming gloves off and got to his feet.

"Take over Ash – I'm being slaughtered," he said casually.

Ash looked at Hants. "Do you need me?" he asked.

Hants dismissed him with a brief shake of his head and turned to Flinn.

"What's wrong?" Flinn asked, eyes dark with suspicion, "Nothing's happened has it?"

"We're just hoping you can help us with an inquiry," Hants said. "We need to speak to Clara Slade. I believe you know her."

"Yes." Flinn put his hands in his pockets, "But why are you asking me? Is she all right?"

"We hope so," Hants responded calmly,

"We need to speak to her regarding an incident. We haven't been able to find her and we're concerned for her safety. Have you seen her in the last twenty-four hours?"

"I saw her yesterday," Flinn replied with a frown, "She went home about three o'clock. What sort of incident?"

"We just need to speak to her," Hants repeated evasively, "You haven't heard from her since yesterday afternoon?"

Flinn shook his head slowly. "No."

"If you do hear anything - we would appreciate it if you inform us as soon as possible."

"Sure," he shrugged, but his eyes said he did not entirely trust Hant's explanation, "Is that all?"

"I'd like to have a quick word with Ashley."

"Ash...!"

The boys swapped places again.

"Yeah?" Ash asked suspiciously.

"I would like to have a quick look over the premises, if you don't mind."

The boy seemed to understand that this was not a request.

"Fine," he said, "But you'd better not wake my brother."

Hants went to the front door and signalled to another two officers waiting outside. Taking one upstairs with him, he left the remaining two officers to search the rest of downstairs. It did not take them long to check the house and garden, but there was nothing to be found except a semi-conscious man in his twenties, half naked on the floor of one of the bedrooms.

"Anything?" Hants asked the officers when he returned to the lounge.

"Nothing, sir."

Hants indicated the back room with a raised eyebrow.

"Another boy, sir. I took his name," one of them confirmed. He gave Ash a patronising smile. "Been in a few fights recently, you lot?"

"I hope you don't expect me to answer that," Ash responded bluntly.

"Come on," Hants said, moving towards the door, "Thank you for your time," he added, and let himself out.

*

Clara wrapped the towel around her tired body and stared at her reflection in the mirror above the sink. Her body was grateful for the comforting warmth of the shower, but now she just wanted to curl up and go to sleep and escape the ache in her muscles. Sleep was unlikely though, as her brain was still trying to face the fact that she was losing her life as she had known it.

She had tenderly examined the damage Rocket had done to her torso in the shower, flinching as she remembered the intentional force with which he had struck her. He had known what he was doing, ensuring she would be unable to make the smallest move without triggering the now familiar pain. She also had a tender swelling on her right forearm where his knee had bashed the bone, but the worst-looking injury was to the left side of her face. She could understand the reaction it had drawn from the others. The flesh was swollen and plump with burgeoning bruises across her cheek bone and at the corner of her mouth. She had a permanent sneer on the top left of her lip and a frown on the bottom. The cut in her mouth had stopped bleeding a while ago, but she could feel the rough edge of it with her tongue. Ash was right: anyone glancing at her would see the bruises first and, in the right clothes and context, make assumptions about her gender.

She carefully combed her hair, gave herself a centre parting and allowed the water to trickle from the ends on to her shoulders. In a moment, when she was ready, Ash would cut her hair. He had promised to take off only enough to make it easier to pile up her hair under a hat. As he had reassured her, some boys had long hair too. Clara gathered up her hair and tried holding it up at different lengths - to see what difference it would make and how short it would need to be for her to get away with it.

The truth was, her head was in limbo; she did not want to turn herself in, but she did not feel confident that the best thing to do was go on the run. If she could commit either way, she would be able to make clearer decisions, like not cutting her hair or telling Ash to chop it all off.

She needed to sleep. If she could escape her body and her mind for a while she might be in a fit state to take charge of her future. At the moment she was just going with the plan Ash had suggested: go with the Boarders to the skateboarding event in Hampton, let the trail cool off for a couple of days and then head for the capital. They were going to tell the other Boarders that Clara was running away from her aunt and that she was going to stay with her brother. They would believe it because they would believe Ash.

Clara pulled on the clothes Ash had given her, slipping on Flinn's red hoody as the final layer. It was the only familiar thing she had now, and it would be something meaningful to hold on to after she had left

Flinn, Carver and Ash behind her.

Ash was in the kitchen with a stool and a pair of salon scissors. Flinn had gone to pick up Rosie; so, apart from the hung-over brother upstairs, it was now just Clara and Ash in the house.

"I found these," he said, holding up the scissors, "Must be mum's. Are you ready?"

"Yes." Clara sat herself on the stool, glad there was not a mirror around.

"I'll try not to take too much off," Ash said reassuringly, "And I apologise in advance – I've not cut anyone's hair before, so it's going to be pretty basic."

Clara laughed, touched by his concern. "It's fine. You don't have to do this anyway – any of it." She handed him the comb and he got to work.

"Well," Ash replied vaguely, "You're all right. And if Flinn trusts you, then so do I."

"You'll be in trouble if they think you've knowingly helped someone like me."

"Perhaps."

"If they do catch me," Clara continued, watching feathers of hair falling to the floor out of the corner of her eye, "You should stick to the story you're telling the others. You can say that's what I told you."

"Will do," Ash agreed gravely.

"What will you tell your brother?"

"Nothing. He doesn't know the police

were here. I'll say you're Flinn's girlfriend and you needed a place to stay. He won't mind - might not even notice. We'll be gone tomorrow."

For a moment there was quiet, except for the snip of the scissors as they sliced through her hair. Clara wondered what Jena would make of her now. She wished she could speak to her again, to try and explain and make up. And to warn her. She imagined the police had spun her the vague story they had told Flinn, so as of yet she probably did not know that her friend was a deviant. How would she react to that? She already felt betrayed because Clara had started skateboarding. How would Jena feel knowing that she had kept her deviancy from her?

Clara could only guess at how the Divinity Division had tracked her down; but from what Carver had said, they had been led to Flinn through the skateboarding. Apart from Carver, Jena was the only person who had known about it. Clara did not believe that Jena would use the skateboarding to turn her in to the Divinity Division. Her aunt, on the other hand, would. Somehow she must have found out and made a report.

What bothered Clara the most, however, was whether her parents knew yet. Had they contacted Greg? What would they say? If she disappeared, she would never be able to talk to them and explain. She would never be able to talk to them, ever. She would not know how they felt: if they were disappointed, humiliated or angry, or if they extended the same grace that Flinn and Ash had. Because she was family, would that make them less or more likely to forgive her? Clara could not bear the thought of not seeing them again, but she was not sure if she could face their reaction either.

"Nearly done," Ash said near her ear.

She felt the cold metal of the scissors touch her chin lightly and heard the final snip.

"I think that's it."

Clara tentatively touched her head and ran her fingers through her hair until it stopped at her chin.

"It's a sort of bob, I guess," Ash said, "There's a mirror in the hall…"

Clara eased herself off the stool, glancing down at the carpet of hair on the floor around it, and crept into the hall. She approached the mirror with caution and faced her reflection reluctantly. It was a basic cut, but it would make things a lot easier. She ruffled her hair gently and tucked the front strands behind her ears. She pulled her hood up and looked at herself critically. She could pass for a boy.

"Almost," Ash said from the lounge door.

He made a face to hide his embarrassment: "You need to lose..." He pointed to his own chest and Clara laughed, "And then...," Ash added, undoing the leather band around his wrist, "You just need this."

He took her wrist and fastened the band around it. He glanced her over as an artist examines his work. "There," he said approvingly, "Now you are a Boarder."

Chapter Thirteen

Woodward observed Hants carefully as he stood over the table, several Slates he had commandeered spread out on its surface. The Divinity Agent had been at the station all night waiting for a twitch on the line to show he had caught his deviant. Woodward was a little awed; as far as he knew, Hants had not even taken a moment to sleep. Woodward made that forty-eight hours. That could not be healthy. It could not be human. The DCI cleared his throat gently to announce his presence, but the polite gesture was ignored. He came forward into the room.

"Any luck?" he asked casually.

"Where would you go," Hants replied, "If you were a teenage girl and you needed to hide?"

"To someone I trust," Woodward replied automatically.

"Who would that be?"

The DCI shrugged. "Family?"

"Parents are abroad, brother lives in the capital and she's stuck in the village."

"A friend then."

"But if you were a deviant?"

"I'd hide on my own I guess," Woodward said, admiring the precision of the lines in which Hants had laid out the Slates. They could not have been more evenly spaced if he had used a ruler.

"There's nowhere for her to hide. We've searched every bit of woodland, field and farm with Thermal Imaging Cameras. We would have found her."

"Not if someone else found her first," Woodward commented.

Hants brought up a list on one of the Slates. "One of these?" he mused aloud, "It has to be a friend. Unless a stranger has taken her in."

"You've visited all of these?"

"Yes. Searched their homes too."

"These are all school friends?"

"Mostly - except this one," Hants pointed to one of the names, "Must be from a different school - the name's not on the roll at the local secondary, I already cross-referenced it." Hants paused as if suddenly struck by something.

"What is it?" Woodward asked.

"We don't actually have an address for him either," Hants said thoughtfully. "He was just in one of the houses we visited."

Hants highlighted the name and ran it through the National Identity Database which would match it to anyone in the country with the same name or a close variation of it.

"Hmm," Woodward pondered as the

results came up on the screen. "I assume you were hoping for a teenage boy to come up as a match?"

He glanced at Hants who was showing his teeth in a smile that made Woodward shudder.

"Actually, I was hoping it wouldn't," he said, grabbing the slate and heading to the door.

"Where are you going?" Woodward called after him; but he had gone.

*

Hants did not bother to shut the car door behind him as he got out of the vehicle and took long strides across the untidy lawn to the front door. He banged on the door as several policemen crept round the side of the house.

"Open up!" he called sharply as he heard someone come down the stairs. A man in his twenties opened the door with an angry look.

"Hey!" he exclaimed, as several officers pushed past him. He snarled at Hants who remained on the doorstep.

"Where is your brother?"

"He's not here," came the irritated reply.

"Is there anyone but you in the house?"

"No! What's this about? What do you want with Ash?"

"Where is he? When did he leave?"

"They left about an hour ago. They've gone to Hampton – to some stupid skateboarding event or something."

"By train?"

" 'Course."

Hants did not wait for any more.

There were two squad cars waiting at the station when he arrived.

"A train to Hampton left twenty-seven minutes ago, sir," one of the officers told Hants as they walked to the manager's office, "The guard remembers seeing at least one group of boys with skateboards getting on board."

"I want to see the CCTV footage," Hants said bluntly, "And the ticket seller."

"Yes, sir."

He was shown into a tiny but neat little room, with several screens and telephones on a curved desk. An officer stood in one corner whilst the stationmaster was bent over a keyboard, calling up images on one of the screens. He turned around anxiously when he heard Hants come in, but then continued his rapid tapping on the keys.

"Here we are," he said nervously, "This is the footage of the platform."

Hants stared intently at the screen with a deceptively calm look on his face.

"What are you looking for exactly?" the manager asked tentatively.

"A girl," Hants replied simply, "Who is dressed as a boy."

The manager stared helplessly at the footage. "Umm… do you know what she is wearing?"

"No."

"They…," the manager hesitated, "They all look the same I'm afraid – from this angle."

He was right. There was nothing to see except a group of figures in hoodies and jeans, all carrying skateboards and a rucksack. Most had their hoods pulled over their heads. All indistinguishable from each other: a true herd. Safety in numbers, Hants thought wryly.

"Ticket line?" he asked.

"Again…," the manager said slowly, bringing up the images, "Not much good with the faces…"

"Sir?" a voice said at the door, "The ticket seller, sir."

The ticket seller was shown in and stood confidently to one side, thumbs hooked into his belt as if ready to pour forth some great wisdom.

"You sold tickets for Hampton to the

Boarders?" Hants asked.

"Yes. They bought an open return ticket each."

"And you got a good look at all of their faces?"

"I always remember faces," the man said. "Haven't seen that girl you're looking for though."

"She won't look like a girl," Hants retorted. "She's disguised as a boy - as a skateboarder."

"I'm good with faces," the man said again, bridling a little. "I haven't seen hers - not buying a ticket."

"She might look a little different," Hants said, suddenly remembering a comment made during their visit to Ash Morgan's house the day before. "Did you sell a ticket to a boy who looked as if he had been in a fight?"

"Most of them looked a bit roughed up," the man said, a little bemused, "But there was one with a long bruise down his face, here." He marked a line downwards on his own face, "I remember now - he bought two tickets."

"Two return tickets to Hampton?" Hants clarified.

"Yes."

"That's them," Hants said, turning to the officer standing in the corner, "He bought the ticket for her, to avoid identification." Hants strode out of the office, the policeman following at his heels. "Alert Hampton - they can pick them up at the station. Contact the guard on the train – find out which carriage they're in."

"Yes, sir! Where are you going, sir?" he asked as Hants got back into his car.

"To pick up my deviant," came the short reply.

*

Suburbia flew by: back gardens with swing sets and plastic pools; allotments with rows of runner bean poles and deckchairs set out in the sun; golf courses with red flags stirring in the summer's breeze; and playing fields full of dog walkers and early sunbathers. All this gradually gave way to stretches of dry heathland, some of it blackened by heath fires, and then wooded hills and cuttings, ironically peaceful as the train sped through them. Clara watched it all quietly, feeling the distance growing between her old life and her uncertain future. She was surprised they had got this far without being caught. The rest of the Boarders had accepted their story without any questions, on the principle that you helped your own and distrusted authority.

They bought the idea that Clara would run away from her aunt because her right to choose her friends and her hobbies was being restricted, and since they were the friends she was in trouble for having, they believed they had a duty to protect her. They'd had a bit of fun passing her off as a boy to Ash's brother Sye, and, by the time they got to the station, she was a fully initiated Boarder.

It would not be long now before they got to Hampton. The train was beginning to creep back through stretches of built-up areas.

Clara tucked a loose strand of hair under her hat and glanced along the length of the train, which was almost full with passengers. She knew that there were other Boarders on the train, in small groups or pairs, presumably going to the same event.

The carriage door hissed open as the guard came through, checking the tickets of those who had got on at the last station. He worked his way slowly along the aisle, inspecting each ticket before punching a hole in it. He had already checked theirs when they had got on, so she was surprised when he stopped by their seats again.

"Tickets?"

"You've seen them," Ash said bluntly,

holding his up with a mild gesture of irritation.

" 'Course," the guard mumbled; and Clara caught him giving her a long stare before he moved off.

"What did he want?" Flinn said under his breath.

"Just being a jerk," Ash replied. "It's this," he said, pulling at his own hoody: "Makes them jittery."

Clara glanced at Flinn, sitting opposite her, and saw that he was looking warily down the carriage after the guard. He got up suddenly and squeezed out into the aisle.

"Where are you going?" Ash hissed after him, but he got no response. He turned to Clara. "Are you all right?"

"He looked at me funny," Clara said thoughtfully.

"The guard? He would - you look like a prize boxer."

"Thanks," she replied dryly. "Seriously, Ash - why would he ask for our tickets again?"

"Because we're Boarders. Look, Sye was convinced you were a boy, we had no problem at the station..."

"But what if he was looking for a boy," Clara said. An inkling of suspicion was growing in her gut, which she could not ignore.

"Why would he?"

"I don't know – how many stops before Hampton?"

"One more, I think."

Clara did not say anything for a while, but let her mind churn with the rhythm of the train, her middle finger steadily tapping against her thumb on the table in front of her. She did not notice Flinn come back, until he grabbed her ticking hand and sat down.

"Where did you go?" Ash asked.

"The guard asked the other Boarders for their tickets too – the ones who got on with us."

"So?"

"Something's not right." Flinn looked at Clara with serious blue eyes, "I think they're looking for you. I think they know you're with us."

They sat in silence for ten pensive minutes until a mechanical female voice announced: "The next station is Sourwood."

Ash suddenly pulled out his phone and selected a number. They heard it ring as the train began to slow. Ash switched it to speakerphone and placed it on the table between them.

"Yes?" a voice picked up.

"Sye?"

"Yeah, listen mate – now's not a good

time. I've got the boiler man here..."

Ash hung up and got to his feet.

"Yep," he said, grabbing his skateboard and slinging his pack on his back, "Let's go!"

The train hissed to a halt and Clara and Flinn followed Ash's example and headed to the doors.

"Hey! Where're you going?" Radley called as they passed.

"Nowhere," Flinn shot back vaguely as they squeezed past the other passengers and reached the open doors. They hurried on to the platform and headed straight to the gate.

They watched the train pull away again from the car park.

"What was that about?" Flinn asked.

"The boiler man," Ash explained, "It's our code for the police."

"How original."

"Yeah, but it works," Ash smirked, taking the back off his phone and removing the battery. "You'd better do the same." he said to Flinn.

"You've done this before," Clara said.

He grinned at her. "I've just watched too many films. Come on – it won't take them long to work out we got off early and where."

"Where are we going?" Flinn asked, slipping the pieces of his phone into a pocket.

Ash looked at Clara. "What do you reckon? It's your getaway."

Clara looked at them and then down at herself: in Ash's jeans, Flinn's hoody and one of his old skateboards in her hand.

"How far is Hampton?"

"About ten miles."

"Then I think we should go where there are other Boarders. It'll give them a harder time looking for us."

It was the most plausible excuse she could think of, but, really, there was something telling her that Hampton was where she needed to be. At some point she would have to separate from Ash and Flinn, and it would be easier if it were somewhere surrounded by others just like them. She knew the Divinity Division would still look for her at the event; they would not be thrown off by her early jump from the train. The longer she ran, however, the more she felt her future pulling her the other way. It was her promise to Carver that kept her running: that, and spending just a little more time with Flinn. She wanted to have the chance to explain properly to him. She did not want him wondering if she was crazy, as she had wondered about Mr Summers. She wanted Flinn to know that she was the same person, and she just needed the opportunity to tell him why and how. She was not going to quit until she had that.

*

If Hants was growing frustrated, there was no sign of it. His face remained largely expressionless, except for something of a sharp flash in his green eyes, but there was nothing else to suggest any feeling was lurking behind his immaculate exterior. Anyone aware of the situation might admire his patience and self-control, imagining a turmoil of vexation and panic swirling beneath the surface. The truth was, however, that every time Hants was thwarted, he got a sense of satisfaction. He enjoyed the chase and the game of trying to get one step ahead, because not for a moment did he doubt he would be the victor in the end. His deviant might have got off the train early, but he knew whom she was with and where they were going. He just needed a better trap and a pawn to set it. All he had to do now was select the right pawn.

The Boarders had been quietly self-assured in the holding room, until Hants walked in and paced up the line. They could tell instantly that he was not an ordinary policeman or inspector. Having gone up the line once, Hants then came back down it again, stopping only twice to point out two.

Marty and Radley, the two selected boys, were led into separate interview rooms. Hants started with the latter.

"Please state your name for the record."

"Radley Parker."

"You are going to a skateboarding event here in Hampton?"

"Doesn't look like it now," came the hostile reply.

"With a group of friends?"

No response except a narrow look. Hants continued as if he had not noticed.

"Three of those 'friends' you got on the train with, got off the train early - at Sourwood. Correct?"

"Is that a crime?" came the cynical reply.

"Flinn Raize, Ash Morgan and Clara Slade. Those were the three?"

"We don't have girls in our group."

"Yet a girl got on the train with you: this girl... I am showing the interviewee a photograph of Clara Slade."

"No one who looked like that," Radley sneered, "We're all boys."

"And one girl disguised as a boy."

"If she's disguised as a boy, how would I know she's a girl?"

"Are you aware," Hants continued, undeterred, "That it is an offence to harbour or aid a deviant in any way."

"Only one that's broken the Divinity Laws," Radley added calmly.

"That's correct. Are you aware that Clara Slade, who got on the train with you, dressed as one of you, is wanted for breaking the Divinity Laws?"

Radley's expression screwed up in disbelief. "I don't know what you're saying," he said, "But Clara Slade is not a deviant and she did not get on the train with us."

"You do know her then?"

"Yeah. Pretty blonde girl. Can skate apparently. Not a Boarder though – we don't have girls in our group. And she's not a deve. You're trying to tell me that she painted that crazy stuff on the halfpipe? No way!"

"That's exactly what I'm saying," Hants confirmed, "She's been lying to you and your friends, and now she's used you to escape the law – and anyone who's helped her in that will be prosecuted."

"You're wrong," Radley told him, matter-of-factly, "Clara's not a deve. And even if she was – she did not get on the train with us."

Hants did not waste any more of his time. He left the boy to think it over, making it clear the interview was not yet finished, and tried the next teenager.

"Please state your name for the record."

"Marty Gorgan-Leigh."

"You are going to a skateboarding event here in Hampton?"

"That was the plan," came the smirked reply as the boy folded his arms.

"With a group of friends?"

"Yeah."

"Three of those 'friends' you got on the train with, got off early at Sourwood. Correct?"

"So you say," Marty replied.

"Flinn Raize, Ash Morgan and Clara Slade – they were with you on the train and then got off early?"

"I dunno," Marty shrugged vaguely.

Hants gave the tabletop a thoughtful look for a moment and then, gazing up calmly at the boy, said: "Are you aware it is an offence, for which you will be prosecuted, to harbour a deviant?" His tone was mild, as if he were merely mentioning it as a casual fact that might be of interest.

"What's that got to do with anything?" Marty snorted.

"It's got to do with the fact I could charge you with that very offence right here and now." He sat back patiently.

"What are you talking about?" Marty asked carefully, "Why are you talking about a deviant?"

"The girl," Hants said simply, "Clara

Slade. I'm talking about her."

"She's not a deve," Marty scoffed uneasily, "She's just running away from home."

"Is that what she told you?"

"Yeah, of course…" His assured tone was cracking and underneath it was fear; all Hants had to do was pluck at that fear a little more.

"She lied."

"No. Ash said she was just running from her aunt. Ash wouldn't lie."

"She lied to Ash. She's a deviant. We've already collected evidence against her." Hants leant forward again and put his phone on the table, "I am now showing the interviewee a photograph of the Greylinghurst halfpipe. You see that – that is her graffiti. Clara Slade is a deviant. She has lied to all of you and worse than that, she has dragged you all into her crime – Ash and Flinn especially. She's using you." He let that sink in.

"She's a deviant?" Marty repeated, stunned.

"You were aware there was a deviant in Greylinghurst?"

"Well, we figured there must be with the graffiti… It can't be her. She skateboards – she's like one of us…"

"No, she's not," Hants said gravely. "She's been pretending to be one of you – but only for her own agenda. Do you understand that she has got your friends, particularly Ash and Flinn, into potentially very serious trouble?"

"They don't know about her," Marty said, still overwhelmed. "They don't know she's a deve." His shock switched suddenly to anger: "That bitch!"

Hants stood up. There it was: what he needed. There was a small flicker of satisfaction in his eyes: "Interview terminated."

*

Hampton's centre was awash with the tides of Saturday shoppers. Waves of people, sweating in the hot sun, moved like part of a large, organic being across the pedestrianised high street. There were bare arms and legs, abdomens and backs everywhere as people hurried from one air-conditioned shop to another. Clara watched enviously as a pair of young women breezed past her in cotton dresses and flip-flops. She felt the sweat trickle down her breastbone under the bandage she had wrapped around her chest. She was going to evaporate in a minute, but she dare not take off the hoody in case it left her too exposed. They stopped under the shade of some slim trees growing down the centre of the street and checked their bearings.

"We're nearly there," Ash said, peering down the street and then at the directions he had scrawled on the back of his hand, from a passer-by. "If we take a left down there… and then follow the road all the way round…"

"Let's follow them," Flinn suggested. He pointed out four Boarders, unique in the fleshy crowd with their fully-clothed limbs, who were heading in the direction Ash had indicated.

"Better yet," Ash smiled, "Let's join them."

He hurried them after the group and tactfully caught their attention. Ash was easy-going and easy to talk to; with a clear goal in common, they were quickly accepted into the group. They were soon certain they were going the right way when they saw other groups and pairs of Boarders ahead of them, some riding their skateboards along the edge of the road. The route took them away from the town centre and towards an old market near the quay. A couple of banners on railings directed them to some large concrete buildings backing on to a park. A sign screwed above the entrance to the central building announced that this was the 'Tail-Devil Skateboarding Festival', and a less impressive notice directed them to the registration area inside.

A couple of young men and a young woman were sat behind some trestle tables where they were taking names and handing out identity bands. Clara gave the name Flinn had suggested to a guy with a red goatee and brown hair that twisted out of his head as if he had been wired up to an electric current. He scrawled down the name and slapped a band around her wrist.

"You're in bunk five. If you want to put down for any competitions, sign up at the relevant arena. There's your map. Big Show is at eight."

Clara took the map and joined Ash and Flinn.

"Well, we made it," she said with more relief than she felt, "Now what?"

"I wonder if the others are here," Ash said with parental concern.

"They'll be fine," Flinn assured him, "We'll find them tomorrow. Think you can survive an afternoon without your brood?"

"Won't have to - stuck with you two," Ash returned. "I'm starving. I swear I can smell burgers..."

"All right, let's get something to eat and then find a practice park," Flinn suggested. He gave Clara one of his typical smiles. "Time for another lesson?"

The practice parks were small areas, one on either side of the site, that had basic ramps, grind rails and a halfpipe each for festival attendees to use. There were several arenas with larger, more complicated layouts inside the bigger buildings, and a huge open-air arena purpose-built for the event in the middle of the park which backed on to the old market. Around this arena were other roped off areas for other activities: there was a workshop for skateboard repairs and adjustments, a stall selling clothes, an area where you could try trampboarding and swingboarding, and even a slalom course for longboards. After getting some lunch and having a look around the site, they went to the west side practice park and watched the other Boarders for a while.

Clara was impressed by the etiquette there seemed to be between the skaters. Considering the number of skateboarders doing numerous moves and tricks in a relatively small area, there were no collisions or confrontations of any sort. Everyone seemed aware of the others around them, waited their turn or gave way to other Boarders if necessary.

Whilst Ash went straight out on to the park, Flinn encouraged Clara to revisit what he had taught her. The satisfaction of still being able to do everything he had instructed her outweighed the ache it caused in her stomach every time she moved. She was going to miss this.

When he was satisfied, Flinn led her on to the halfpipe at one end. He took a helmet out of his backpack.

"I only brought this," he said.

"You're finally going to let me skate on a halfpipe?"

"This one is quite shallow, so you should be all right."

"Better be," she said good-humouredly, "Or between Rocket and skateboarding I'm going to have a pretty collection of injuries."

Flinn just smiled and handed her the helmet.

"Right," he said, once she had fastened it under her chin and adjusted the strap. "You start off on the flat. Just get used to the feel of it - slide gently a little way up each curve." He put his board down and showed her. "You'll have to 'pump' to get up the sides. Just bend your knees in the flat and straighten as you reach the curve."

He continued opposite her as she copied him. She could feel the extra push and speed created by pumping. There was something soothing and almost therapeutic about the rhythm of the board as it rolled from one side of the pipe to the other, just a little further up the walls each time.

"All right?" Flinn asked, as she got the hang of it.

"Yes. Pretty easy," she agreed.

"Good. To the platform then."

"What do I do if I reach the other side?" Clara asked, standing on the platform with her heart thumping and her palms sweaty. This was more nerve-wracking than the first time she had been about to roll down a halfpipe on a skateboard.

"Turn before you reach the lip," Flinn said, calm and cool as always. "And come back the other way. When you want to get off, stop pumping. The board will slow down and you can dismount as usual."

"Right," she said vaguely.

"You'll be fine. Trust your balance and don't overthink it. Just feel it – and enjoy it."

"Enjoy it," Clara repeated to herself.

Without further hesitation and before she could change her mind, she tipped over the edge of the platform.

Clara left almost everything behind her the moment she went over the lip and down into the bowl of the pipe: her pain, her losses and fears. The only thing she took with her was her heart, pumping with blood and adrenaline in a moment of abandonment. There was only the pipe, the board and her, and the communion of movement between them. She fell in love with the movement, the feeling of lightness and the thrill. Every time she topped the curve and carved round; every time she could have fallen and did not, she felt unstoppably alive.

It seemed an age before she noticed Flinn watching her still, from the platform, hands resting in the pockets of his hoody. She remembered his tip and stopped pumping, allowing the board to slow and eventually stop on the flat of the pipe.

Flinn climbed down to join her. She took off the helmet and readjusted her hat.

"Pretty good," Flinn said.

Clara rubbed her stomach where the muscles were complaining. She handed the helmet to him. "Your turn, teacher."

He took the helmet with a smirk, put it on and went to the top of the halfpipe. Clara sat on one of the benches to watch, hugging her stomach with one arm and resting her chin on the other hand. She watched as Flinn took to the halfpipe as if he had been born on four wheels. She wished this was her life. This would be simpler: just the skate park, Boarders and nothing to overcome except the hazards of the halfpipe. But this was not her life and it never would be. She did not know what her life was going to be instead. No matter how many times she ran Carver's words through her mind, something told her that this extra time she had stolen was not for long. Something was coming that she could not stop; and this time she had now, this chance to catch a breath in the race, was her last chance to set things right with Flinn.

She remembered his reaction that night he had caught her and how he had withdrawn from her: cut her off. And although he had revoked his initial response, he was still avoiding the rift that had cracked open in their friendship. He had not asked her to explain anything. He had just helped her without question and without understanding either. Clara wanted to explain everything to him. She needed to explain, or he would forever have two versions of her that he could not reconcile: the nice village girl and the deviant. She could see it whenever she caught him looking at her. He was wondering what she was, really - what he still did not know about her.

But she did not know how to tell him. She did not have the words to make him understand fully what she knew and what she felt. If he asked, it would be easier; but she did not know that he ever would. Perhaps she could write it down. It might be her only way of saying goodbye too. When they caught her, she was not going to be allowed to see anyone.

If they caught her, she corrected herself. If she did not manage to disappear.

Ash came and joined her. "I think we should get to our bunk and claim a spot – it's going to get even busier later."

Clara nodded in agreement. "Have you still got that pen?" she asked.

"Sure." He fished in his pocket and handed it to her. He made a signal to Flinn, who skated smoothly off the park, helmet under one arm.

"Bunk down?" Ash suggested.

"Sure," Flinn nodded.

"Then dinner."

"All you think of is your stomach."

"It's hungry work being the brains of this outfit."

They headed towards the buildings allocated as accommodation. It was a very basic system: you were given a bunk number which corresponded to a section of one of the old market barns, partitioned off with corrugated iron walls. Each bunk could take up to thirty people in its rectangular concrete space. You picked a spot, rolled out your sleeping mat and that was then your sleeping quarter. The three of them set up in a corner of Bunk Five, grabbing as much space as they could as they spread out the mats and sleeping bags.

"It's not very comfortable," Ash apologised, "Or private. But it's bearable for a couple of nights."

Clara looked down at her mat against the wall, barely offering an inch of protection from the cold concrete floor. Then she glanced across at the two other mats with their sleeping bags next to hers - buffers against the strangeness of the space. It was considerably better, in many ways, than a police cell.

"I reckon," Ash said, "I get us something to eat, bring it back here, and then we go to see the Big Show at eight." He looked thoughtfully at the two of them for a moment. "You both stay here – make sure no one moves our stuff."

Flinn and Clara made themselves comfortable whilst they waited for Ash. Flinn took a pack of playing cards from his rucksack and they played a couple of easy games. If ever Flinn was going to ask, this was his opportunity. There was only one other group in the bunk and they were in the opposite corner, so they could have talked without being overheard. But Flinn did not ask. They talked about the festival, the Big Show that evening where the pros would show off their skills; about the number of Boarders; what they had seen of Hampton;

Ash and the others: everything but the reason she was here. They managed, without trying, to avoid anything that might lead to that topic. And Clara did not push Flinn on it: not just because there was a Divinity Law preventing her, but because she knew it had to come from Flinn. If he did not want to know, then she would not be able to explain. Until he asked, her lips were sealed.

Ash brought back fish and chips, which they devoured whilst they watched more Boarders join them in the bunk. Clara suddenly felt very tired. She was struggling to stay tuned in to the conversation; and she could feel herself curling inwards, withdrawing like a tortoise does, into her own private world. She tried hard to stay alert, but she had not slept for two nights, even though Ash's sofa had been comfortable. She had lain awake, staring at the lamplight through the curtains, replaying the last few weeks of her life.

"Clara?" Flinn asked gently, "Are you all right?"

She smiled reassuringly. "Yes. I'm just tired. I think I'll skip the show, if you don't mind?"

"Sure." he hesitated for a second, "Will you be all right on your own?"

"Yes. You go."

"Sure?" Ash frowned, "What if... there's a problem?"

"I'll be okay," Clara assured him, "If there's a problem I'll be able to disappear quite easily. I might as well stay here and look after our stuff."

Neither of them looked very easy about it, but they got to their feet eventually.

"You can leave the cards," Clara smiled, grabbing them before Flinn could.

He smiled back. "All right, but I won't be impressed if we come back to a poker tournament." He glanced round them one more time, before giving her an uneasy look. "Won't be long," he promised.

"I'll be fine."

He nodded. She gave a mock salute and watched them leave the bunk. Then she took Ash's pen and the map of the site from her pocket and laid them out on the mat in front of her. The back of the map was blank, but it was only A5 sized, so she would have to use the space wisely and choose her words with care.

When she had finished, she folded the paper neatly and slipped it into the pack of cards, and then put it back into Flinn's rucksack. Hopefully, he would find it, at the right time, after she had gone. It did not explain everything, there was not enough room, but it was a goodbye - in case she did not get the chance later.

It was still quite early, and as she was alone now in the bunk and tired, Clara crawled into her sleeping bag and curled up on the mat with her back to the wall. For a long time she just lay and listened to the echoes of the barn, the distant footsteps and voices from another bunk, the gurgling of a pipe and the muffled thump of music carried from the park. She felt homesick for the sounds of her home: the familiar breathe and creak of floorboards, her dad's gentle cough as he cleared his throat, the sigh of the stairs as her mum came up to bed. As the cold nausea of knowing you are cut off from where you belong sank into her stomach, she would have given anything to be home with her family again. How could she live a life without them? How could she go into a life where she would be cut off from them indefinitely? Did she have any other choice? The only other option was the rehabilitation camp. She remembered Carver's words: "They break you down bit by bit. Don't think they'll let you out if you still have the spark..."

She had a hard choice to make. And tomorrow she would have to make it: either she would get it right or she would get it wrong – but either way, there would be no going back.

*

Marson's frown was now permanent, his forehead furrowed by the knit of his eyebrows. Hants could tell he was desperate for some good news.

"Well?" he asked.

"I've identified the deviant," Hants told him matter-of-factly.

"So I heard. Where is she?"

"I have her location," Hants confirmed. "I know she is in Hampton – at the 'Tail-Devil Skateboarding Festival'."

"Good. Are you going to pick her up tonight?"

"No, sir," Hants replied calmly, "There's too great a risk of losing her at night. It would be easy for her to disappear at the festival and we don't yet have a definite location on the site for her. She could be anywhere at any time. I have got an insider who will make contact tomorrow morning with a more precise location."

"Just make sure you do get her tomorrow, Hants," Marson said gravely. "I need you back on the underground cases, and we need this one wrapped up." He gently rubbed the knot in his brow with a sigh. "There's been a considerable rise in blackwashings this month. I don't know if we're just having more success at catching deviants, if they're being more careless, or if their numbers are simply growing."

Hants made no response, either to encourage or to offer an opinion. Marson stopped rubbing his brow and looked at his agent.

"Just let me know when you have her in custody."

"Yes, sir."

"It has to be tomorrow, Hants."

Hants did not smile, but there was a confident twitch at the corner of his mouth. "It will be, sir. I guarantee it."

Chapter Fourteen

Flinn was on edge. He had been on edge all day and it had amplified his senses. The boom of the music being pumped around the park was like thunder to his ears, the roll of wheels and scraping of decks grated on his nerves, and the crowds of Boarders milling around the site had become a hurricane of chaos he was struggling to negotiate. He snarled as yet another hoodied figure bumped his arm and drew a look of surprise from Ash. Flinn had been in enough tricky situations to recognise his flight or fight instinct kicking in. The trouble was he did not know what he was fighting or fleeing yet, and that made him more restless.

It had been a normal day so far, and nothing had happened to cause any worry. After a late start they had watched the first competition at Arena A, grabbed brunch, watched Ash try trampboarding and then been to a practice park. Now they were on their way to meet up with Clara again, who had gone to the bunk whilst Flinn had the front truck of his board fixed. Ash had come along to see if he could scout out the others, but so far he'd had no luck.

"You all right?" Ash asked quietly, giving him a quick, careful glance out of the corner of his eye.

"Fine," Flinn lied coolly.

"Ash!" a voice cut through the crowd, rather desperately, "Ash!"

Flinn stopped dead and turned with Ash to see Marty and Radley pushing through the crowd to meet them.

"Ash, Flinn...," Marty said breathlessly, "Where've you been?" His look was a little accusatory and nervous. "I've been looking for you." His gaze ran over them and then slid around to scan the crowd, as if he was expecting to see someone else.

Flinn fixed a look on him and stayed back, trying to calm the pounding in his chest as Ash stepped forward.

"Sorry, Mart," Ash said, giving him a light slap on the shoulder, "We had some business to attend to. Where've you all been?"

"They pulled us in," Radley said grumpily, "We only got out this morning. They called our parents."

Ash raised his eyebrows. "Who did?"

"The police," Radley muttered.

"Or more precisely, the Divinity Division did," Marty added, "Where's the girl?"

"Clara?" Ash responded calmly, "Back at our bunk."

"Which bunk are you in?" Marty asked, "We were lucky to get a bunk this morning. We're over in twelve. Where are you?"

Ash folded his arms and planted his feet

apart a little. It was such a subtle movement that Marty paid no attention to the fact that Ash was now half-covering Flinn, who still stood a step behind listening to the conversation in silence.

"Five," Ash answered simply. "What's going on? Why were the Double D interested in you?"

"They're after the girl," Marty said, lowering his voice slightly. "Ash - she's a deve. She's been taking us - you - for a ride. They wanted to charge us for harbouring a deviant. I told them we knew nothing about her being a deve."

Ash looked thoughtful for a moment.

"Is she still with you?" Radley asked softly.

Ash looked at them both as if he was not sure they were talking about the same thing. "Are you saying Clara is a deve?"

"Yes," Marty said, sounding a little exasperated, "Is she still with you guys?"

"Yes," Ash responded slowly.

"Where is she?" Marty pressed. "At the bunk? Bunk five?"

Ash gave him a funny look. "Well, let's find out."

Radley caught his eye with a quiet look, and then Marty voiced what they had both deliberately not brought his attention to. He looked around at the crowd that swept past them, a look of naïve confusion on his face. "Where's Flinn?"

*

Flinn remembered why Ash was such a good friend when he had sidestepped in front of him, cutting him off from the conversation. As soon as Marty mentioned the Divinity Division, they did not have to look at each other to confirm their time was up. Now that the others knew about Clara, there would be divided opinions on what should be done about her. They could not play dumb now and pretend they did not know what she was, and they could not afford for anyone to suspect they had willingly helped someone they knew to be a deviant. So they could not lie anymore. It was time for Clara to disappear on her own. She just needed someone to warn her, to give her a head start.

Flinn had not waited more than a few seconds after Ash had given up their bunk number. Then he had turned smoothly and joined the crowd. He had started at a walk, so as not to draw any attention, but then he had started to run, until he was sprinting towards the old market buildings.

There were a few groups milling about as he darted through the bunks to number five, but no one paid him any attention. Clara was sitting cross-legged on her mat and looked up calmly as he dropped his board next to her.

"Time to go!" he said simply.

She read the look on his face and, without saying anything, got to her feet. Flinn grabbed her by one arm.

"This way."

They walked quickly out of the back of the building, where a narrow path ran alongside the park fence. They crossed the path and vaulted easily over the railings. Flinn glanced quickly from left to right and hissed between his teeth. Clara followed his gaze and saw a couple of police officers running up the narrow path they had just left. The officers' eyes were on the old building she and Flinn had just evacuated, and it was clear they had escaped just in time. A few seconds later and it would have been a different story.

"That was close," Clara breathed.

Flinn tugged at her arm and they began weaving at a quick pace through the crowds. As they neared the main arena, the soup of people thickened and slowed as Boarders piled up for the next show. They received a few annoyed looks as they shouldered their way through, past the arena where the flow of people thinned again. As they emerged from the stagnation of bodies, Flinn glanced to his left to check his bearings. A neatly-dressed man, who stood out from the crowd in his suit and tie, turned at the same time and recognised him. The man's cool gaze travelled across to Clara, as she glance round to follow Flinn's stare, and there was a moment of mutual identification.

"Shit," Flinn said, "It's that agent."

Clara suddenly came to life. Taking the initiative, she grabbed Flinn's sleeve and ran, cutting a line across the grass, through groups lounging in the sun, over a bench and through a group having some sort of skate-off. She was surprisingly light-footed. A check over his shoulder showed Flinn that Clara's direct approach had given them a significant lead on the agent already. Flinn caught sight of him, following cautiously after them, his mouth moving as he issued instructions into his mouthpiece. At his steady but slow pace he obviously was not planning on chasing them himself, and this was confirmed when a glance across the park revealed two uniformed officers sprinting in their direction.

"We've got more company…," Flinn muttered.

Clara threw a glance over her shoulder and then nodded ahead of them. Flinn saw the sign to the east side practice park in the near distance.

"Think you can handle it?" Clara asked, and she actually smiled.

Flinn grinned back, "You're crazy!" He shrugged. "I'm up for it if you are."

Clara released her grip on his sleeve as they reached the entrance to the park, and jumped over the spectators' benches. The whole park was a mêlée of rushing wheels, figures twisting mid-air, sliding along grind rails and carving across the tarmac. The risk of a painful collision whilst on a skateboard was high enough, but being hit by a skater as a pedestrian would almost certainly mean broken bones.

Don't think about it, Flinn told himself, as they ran. Don't overthink it. Just go with it and you'll be fine. Probably. He tried to keep his eyes and mind on the other side of the park, but his muscles flinched at the anticipation of impact. Although he was the faster sprinter, Clara was ahead of him, and he could not help but marvel at how agile she was on her feet. She negotiated grind rails, ramps and skateboarders like a cat, not once hesitating or losing her balance.

Flinn only realised he had been holding his breath after they leapt over the wall on the other side of the park and the air rushed out of his lungs in a sigh of relief. On the other side of the wall was a steep bank of flowerbeds and beyond that, the railing, which separated the park from the street. Halfway up the bank, Flinn checked behind and saw one police officer had collided with a skateboarder, while the other was shouting into his mouthpiece as he skirted around the practice park.

Flinn grabbed the railings, pulled himself over and narrowly missed being hit by a car as he darted across the road after Clara. He caught up with her and grabbed her arm. They were on a straight road of posh-looking offices, lined with young trees along the pavement as an attempt at gentrifying the area. They had to get off of this street and somewhere less open and exposed.

There was a busy main road at the end of the street and a subway entrance, which they immediately headed towards. They pounded down the steps without pausing - through the darkness of the tunnel, and up the other side - and found themselves in a more residential area of block flats and terraced houses.

They did not stop running until they had taken several turns into the estate, and dived into a quiet side road of garages. They stopped against a wall to catch their breath.

"Do you think they're following?" Clara

asked, wincing as she caught her breath and held her side.

"Don't know," Flinn admitted. He glanced at her as she leant with her back against the wall, staring into space as she tried to regain control of her lungs. She had lost her hat and her face looked pale underneath the blush and bruising on her cheeks.

"Ever thought of taking up free-running?" he asked.

She laughed shortly. "I thought it was going to be death by skateboarder."

"How long?" Flinn asked after a pause. She gave him a puzzled look, so he continued quickly: "How long have you been a… you know?"

Clara took a few slow, deep breaths before answering. "A couple of months."

"Did Summers turn you?"

She shook her head. "No. I was already there. He just… we just discovered each other."

"Did you know Carver was one too?"

"No." She smiled wryly. "Funny really – all that time, he was right next door."

"You didn't know it was his graffiti?"

Clara shrugged. "I knew it was another – deviant."

"And that's why you painted the rest? To let him know you were there too?"

"Yeah. Partly," she assented, as she crept

to the corner of the building and peered back down the street. She drew back again and looked at him steadily. "I guess I just wanted anyone to know I was there – that I existed."

" 'Here I am,' " Flinn agreed.

The quiet was suddenly ripped by a siren.

"Time to go again!"

*

Hants spotted DCI Woodward at the park gate and inwardly rolled his eyes. So now everyone was interested in his deviant; now that it had become a chase across town, it was worth their attention.

"This investigation of yours is turning into a bit of a farce," were Woodward's first words to him. "Been given the run around by a teenager, eh?"

"I have someone to chase," Hants replied coolly. "Less than a week ago you didn't even believe she existed."

"Bet you thought you'd have her in a cell by now though?" Woodward said, bristling a little at the comment and overcompensating with a sneer that came out rather sulkily.

"I'll have her in a cell by the end of the day," Hants said matter-of-factly.

"Yeah?" the DCI half closed one eye and restrained a cynical smile. "How do you know that for certain?"

"She hesitated."

"Huh?"

Hants smiled inwardly at Woodward's puzzled expression. The DIC did not know, and could not understand, how to read a deviant at a glance. But Hants did; and when his gaze had met that of his deviant, she had hesitated. She had looked at him, and she had instantly known who he was. And yet she had shown a moment of indecisiveness. Hants had chased enough deviants to know the difference between one who was merely running and one who was escaping. And this one was not escaping.

It had only been for a second, but he had seen it in those grey eyes: a flicker of recognition, like a person who has seen their fate every night in a dream and then one day turns round and finds it staring them in the face. Her sudden flight was instinct, duty, what made sense in that moment of confrontation. Hants had seen it plenty of times. Some deviants wanted to escape; they were determined not to be caught and they went to every length they could to ensure their freedom: they did not hesitate. And then there were others who did not want to escape. They wanted to be caught, to be found, to be known. They wanted the freedom, not of a new life without bars and locks, but of a life free from pretending and hiding. They wanted to freely be what they were, despite the consequences. They were the ones who would go to the gallows, the pyre or the lions' den rather than deny their true nature. They would choose to die free rather than live fettered by fear.

That's why Hants knew he would find her, because she wanted him to find her. Really, deep down, she did not want to run.

So Hants faced Woodward's scepticism with confidence. "What are you doing here?" he asked. "This is not your jurisdiction."

"No. But she's my criminal. She deviated on my patch, so I thought I'd better make sure she ends up in my station. That's where I've got her parents waiting."

Hants' eyes narrowed in surprise. "That was a quick return."

"Apparently they were on their way back. Something about an email from the aunt that got them worried. They got in this morning. So," he added with a large intake of breath, "What are you going to do to catch this girl then? She could be anywhere."

"There are patrols out. That should restrict their movement. And then, when it starts to get dark and there are less people about, we'll call the 'copter out."

"What for?"

"Thermal imaging."

"That could pick up anyone."

Hants refrained from an expression of impatience. "They'll be hiding somewhere isolated – away from people – because, by then, my deviant's face will have been all over the local news. They won't want to be spotted in public."

"You're assuming they'll be outside. If they've found somewhere to hide, you'll never find them."

"If they're in a building, it will be an empty one – somewhere quiet. That at least narrows our search a little."

Woodward shrugged and then frowned. "They? Why 'they'?"

"She's got a friend with her. He probably doesn't know she's a deviant. He's not a concern – as long as we get the girl."

"He might be a deviant too," Woodward suggested.

Hants did make a little impatient gesture this time. "When we catch him, you can ask him."

Woodward snorted. "You don't expect him to admit it."

Hants' lips parted in a half smile. "If he's a deviant, he will. That's one thing you'll learn very quickly – deviants never lie about *that*. Ask them anything to do with their deity, the divine and their belief in it, and they'll either spill their souls or say nothing." His tone darkened a little as he carefully emphasised his words: "But they'll never lie."

*

For a while, they had crept through alleys; following meandering back streets through residential areas, and avoiding the blue lights and sirens of patrols. No one paid them much attention, and then soon there were no longer many people around to notice them, as everyone turned homeward for dinner. Eventually, they found a secluded spot, around the back of a small nursery school, and sat for a while in silence, waiting as the evening descended and the air grew chill and soft with the gentle flush of a pink sunset. It was a peaceful place to pass the time, sat against the boundary wall - where a line of cherry trees on the other side sheltered them from the street. They had a view of a glass classroom door, which was covered in child-drawn pictures of unidentifiable creatures. Above their heads, a blackbird called out repetitively to the growing twilight.

"You said you could graffiti," Flinn said suddenly, "For your Art project."

Clara turned her head to meet his blue eyes as they searched her face.

"Was that your way of telling me it was you..?"

"It was the closest I was going to get," she admitted.

"Were you going to tell anyone?"

Clara thought for a moment, as if trying to decide whether that was information she should share. And then she glanced up, and Flinn copied her, as a sound reached them through the air. It was a distant sound, but quite distinctive all the same.

"Is that..?" Clara began.

"It's a helicopter," Flinn confirmed, getting carefully to his feet.

"Do you think it's for us?"

He crinkled his nose at the idea. "Possibly. We should get inside a building, just in case."

Clara slowly stood up and followed Flinn to the front of the nursery and back over the gate they had come in by. They walked a couple of miles, keeping on a line away from the town centre, and soon left the inner estates and entered the more industrial areas. They crossed side roads and courtyards lined with warehouses; factories with flat roofs and locked-down garages that had once been brightly painted, but were now faded and stained with rust; dark-windowed offices where buildings were covered with company names and logos; and roads signposted with warnings over parking restrictions and lorries turning.

Eventually they came across a disused glass factory, standing dark and empty in the elbow-crook of a dead end road. There were three forgotten skips outside, full of the innards of the factory. It had obviously been empty for a while and broken into at least once, as evidenced by a shattered ground floor window.

Clara waited near the skips as Flinn scouted out a safe way in. She could still hear the helicopter searching over the town, a red and white flickering light in the darkening sky marking its position. Nearby, a street light came on, spreading a sickly orange glow on the pavement.

The sound of a car suddenly broke the evening stilness and an old jeep turned into the road. Clara watched as it pulled up a little way down the road, and then withdrew herself behind the three skips. She listened tensely to the echo of footsteps up the street towards her and then saw the head and shoulders of a man hover on the other side of the first skip. She stayed where she was, hoping that if she did not move, and he did not come round the skip, he would not see her.

The man grunted a couple of times and shuffled along to the next skip. He paused again and Clara realised he was trying to find room in one of the skips to offload some rubbish.

Finally, he came to the third skip, shuffled awkwardly round the back of it and lifted a cardboard box into the mouth of the container. It landed with a dull clunking sound and the man paused to brush his hands on his trousers. He would have left without noticing her but, as if sensing a presence behind him, he suddenly turned his head in her direction. A look of surprise and guilt crossed his features and then his eyebrows lowered with the suspicion any hooded figure might draw in the darkening evening. He cleared his throat awkwardly and slowly walked back round to the other side of the skip. Out of the corner of her eye, Clara saw his head bob round a second time and peer at her over the content of the container, before he walked back to his car. A moment later, the engine started, she heard the change of gears as he did a three-point turn, and then she was left again in the silence of the gloaming.

She jumped when Flinn put his hand on her elbow.

"Found a way in," he said.

"Found or made?" she asked.

"Better you don't know," he retorted lightly, leading her down the side of the factory to a fire door which was hanging open on one hinge.

Inside, the factory was dark, dusty and completely gutted. Nothing had been left except piles of debris and dirt on the concrete floor. The only light came through the windows at the front, where the light of the street lamps cast an unearthly glow through the dirty glass. Clara shivered against the cold, stale air. She watched Flinn pull the fire door in to a half closed position and then lean against the wall next to it, so he could get a clear view down the side of the factory towards the street. Clara went and positioned herself on the other side of the door and tucked her hands into the front pocket of her hoody.

"They're going to find me," she said, so calm and collected that Flinn felt his heart skip a beat.

"You're not going to get caught."

"There was a man," she added, "Outside. He saw me."

"He won't know who you are or why you're here," Flinn reasoned. "We can always go somewhere else."

"I'm tired, Flinn. I'm tired of running." She was very matter-of-fact about it. "They're going to find me. It's okay. I don't mind."

He looked at her thoughtfully. "I mind."

Clara half laughed. "You should go. I'll be fine. If they catch you with me they'll charge you."

"Probably," he agreed.

"Why didn't you chuck me off the halfpipe that day?" Clara asked, "When I wasn't supposed to be there."

He gave her one of his smiles. "I dunno - you weren't afraid. You should have been, but you weren't – you just looked like you belonged there," he shrugged. "Like you were supposed to be there."

They stood quietly for a moment, Flinn watching the side of the factory with a calm air, both waiting in silent companionship.

"I was going to tell my parents," Clara said after a while.

Flinn's eyes switched to her with an intent expression.

"After they got back from their trip," Clara explained, "I was going to tell them. I thought I could keep it under control until they got back. But then their stay was extended..." She stared ahead of her into the room, and the tone of her voice took on an almost faraway quality, as if she was recounting a dream. "I thought it would be easy to pretend everything was the same – that I was the same. But, once you've got this new thing inside of you – it grows. It has a life of its own – an eternal life. You can't supress it. It won't be supressed," she added a little darkly. "I don't want to suppress it. I don't know how to explain..." She paused, struggling for a second to convey what was still a mystery to her.

In the silence, the thrum of the helicopter grew steadily louder. They deliberately ignored it.

"I guess," Clara said carefully, "It's like an electric fire." She half laughed. "That sounds crazy, but it's close. It's like I've been used to an electric fire and then - out of nowhere - I've found fire - real fire - the thing the electric version has been imitating. And it's hotter, brighter and dangerously unpredictable. It doesn't just provide warmth - it burns. It consumes everything - even you - until you and the flame are one."

She glanced back at Flinn with a smile that was almost apologetic. "Sorry. It's just - I'll never go back. No matter what they do, Flinn - I'll always be fire now. I'll always burn."

The helicopter was overhead now and in the darkness the squeal of racing cars echoed from the estate.

"How did you find it?" Flinn asked. "This 'real' thing...?"

Those grey mirrored eyes searched into his own for a minute whilst car doors slammed and feet pounded outside on the street. "You have to be looking for something to find it," she said finally. "Promise me something, Flinn..."

And then a harsh voice, with a tinny quality, cut through the dark of the factory.

"This is the police! You are surrounded!" it rapped. "You have one minute to vacate the building and turn yourself in or we will come in and get you..."

The voice cut off and a second later another, calmer and smoother voice replaced it.

"This is Agent Hants of the Divinity Division," it said matter-of-factly. "You have thirty seconds to make a decision: you can walk out of the building of your own accord or you can stay where you are and we will come in and get you and anyone else in there with you. Your time starts now."

"Flinn – promise me," Clara said quickly, "You'll deny everything. When they question you – you knew nothing – ever."

"I promise."

"We were friends, yeah?" she said simply.

"We *are* friends," Flinn replied bluntly and suddenly grabbed her wrist and pulled her towards him, wrapping his arm around her shoulders. They held on to each other for a moment as a voice counted down the seconds.

"Come back," Flinn said in her ear, an

unfamiliar tone of desperation in his voice. "Swear you'll come back."

"I will," she promised earnestly.

"Ten seconds… nine… eight…"

Clara pulled away, feeling the wrench inside as he released his hold on her. She slipped through the gap in the door and hesitated.

"Flinn…?"

"Five… four…"

"Yes?"

"Thank you."

*

The officer who was counting down into the megaphone suddenly stopped and Hants saw a movement at the side of the factory. A figure emerged, slow step by slow step, from the gloom and into the lamplight. She stopped a few feet from the line of police officers and took her hands carefully out of the pocket of the red hoody she was wearing.

Hants stepped forward curiously and scanned her up and down for a quiet moment. Her hair was shorter and there was bruising on one side of her face, but this was his deviant. He had forgotten she was only fifteen. Slight of build and fresh-skinned she looked her age, except for a certain mellowness about her manner.

"Clara Slade?" he said matter-of-factly.

"Yes," she replied, looking at him with unafraid grey eyes.

"Wise choice," Hants said, meeting her gaze attentively.

He snapped the cuffs on her wrists. She winced at the click of their closing; the trap had successfully shut.

"Clara Slade, I am arresting you for breaking the Divinity Laws. You have the right to remain silent, but it may harm your defence if you do not mention when questioned something which you later rely on in court. Anything you do say may be given in evidence," Hants reeled off with professional fluency. "Were you alone in that building?"

"Yes," she said. "I am alone."

"What happened to Flinn Raize?"

"I left him."

They looked at each other as Hants signalled to the line of policemen to check the factory. Hants tried to read his deviant: this girl he had flushed out, chased down and finally caught. Here was his mouse. She looked pale and tired, but she was giving him nothing else: no fear, no regret, no anger or defiance. She was perfectly calm, as if she were not really a part of the events unfolding around her. In fact, Hants was looking back at someone as calm and as sure as he was. Those grey eyes were gazing at him as if she could read his thoughts and knew what he would do and say next. For a second Hants felt disempowered. He suspected he had not caught a mouse at all, but another cat. He could not explain it, but he felt he had come to meet an adversary rather than his prey. If he had been asked to draw a battle line, he would have marked it between them, where they stood face to face.

One of the officers returned with a shake of his head. "It's empty, sir."

"Are you sure?"

"Yes, sir. There's no one in there."

"Right then," Hants said, shaking off his uneasy thoughts and inwardly grasping back his authority. "Let's finish this at the station."

Chapter Fifteen

Clara was not prepared for walking in to the station. Everything seemed appallingly real, especially the unfamiliar: the white lights were piercing, the reception area abnormally small, and the smell of coffee and disinfectant offensively pungent. Her senses were so assaulted by the reality of everything around her that she did not recognise the two figures sitting on the chairs, as she came through the doors. It was not until a voice said her name that she stopped in her tracks. It was such a familiar voice and one that she had missed for such a long time that she thought she had imagined it at first. She turned in the direction it had come from and saw, as if in slow motion, her mother already out of her seat and reaching towards her with outstretched arms.

"Clara!" her mother cried again, putting her arms round Clara's neck and squeezing her protectively.

Clara stood stunned for a moment as her father put one hand on her back and gently pressed the side of her face with the other, as he kissed her head. The handcuffs prevented her from grabbing hold of them as she instinctively wanted to, so, instead, she grabbed her mother's jacket in her fists and held on to it as if it were a lifeline.

"My darling," her mother whispered into her ear. "If only we had been here."

"Sir. Madam...," a voice said sternly, "I must ask you to stand aside."

Her mother unwrapped her arms from her neck and touched her bruised face softly. "What happened to you..?" she asked, her eyes searching Clara's sadly. "Who did this?"

"Mr and Mrs Slade...," the officious voice tried again, "I'm afraid you must stand aside..."

A hand grabbed Clara's elbow.

"She's fifteen," her father said. "She should have one of us with her."

"There will be a social worker present," came the reply. "You may be needed as witnesses for the defence. Please, sir... you can speak to your daughter later."

"We'll be right here," her mother said quietly, tucking a strand of hair behind Clara's ear.

Her father planted another kiss on her forehead. "It's going to be all right, darling."

The grip on Clara's elbow tightened and pulled her back. She fixed her eyes on her parents, hardly able to believe that they were really there, and reluctantly allowed the officer to lead her away.

They checked her in, taking her shoes and the contents of her pockets, and then took her to be photographed and fingerprinted. Then she was shown into an interview room. A policewoman brought her a sweet tea and a plate of biscuits. Clara drank the tea gratefully.

Eventually, the door opened and Agent Hants came into the room with another older man and a woman in a red suit. The woman sat on a chair to one side of the table and the older man sat in the chair beside Clara.

"This is Carole Wittacker," Hants said, indicating the woman. "A social worker – she's simply here as an appropriate adult to supervise the interview. And this is Mr Burn, your defence lawyer."

Mr Burn offered Clara his hand. Hants took a seat opposite her.

"You have been cautioned," he began, "Do you understand your rights?"

"Yes."

"And you understand you are charged with breaking the Divinity Laws?"

"All of them?"

Hants smiled at the question. "Specifically the Law of Communication," he clarified. "You are charged with willingly accepting material which references and advocates a belief in the divine. Such material was found hidden in your bedroom." He slid forward several plastic wallets containing the evidence. "I am showing Miss Slade the handwritten texts found in her room. Can you confirm that these belong to you?"

Clara looked at them, carefully spread out on the table, and then up at Hants. "Yes," she said, and added, "That's my handwriting."

"So you admit you copied these texts from printed versions given to you by Hatherhay Summers?"

"You mean Mr Summers, my history teacher?"

"That is correct."

"Yes," Clara agreed without hesitation, "I did."

"Where are the printed versions of the texts that you copied these from?"

"I hid them."

"Where have you hidden them?"

"I hid them," she replied, looking at him with her clear grey eyes, "So that you wouldn't find them."

"Are you refusing to reveal the whereabouts of the illegal documents you have hidden?"

"Yes."

Hants neatly selected one of the plastic wallets as if he were a magician performing a card trick. "Just to confirm, Miss Slade - you are aware that these texts you copied are illegal to possess or read without proper authorisation?"

"Yes."

"And you read and copied these texts because you believe in and adhere to the ideas they express?"

"Yes," Clara asserted. She knew she could speed up this process and avoid having to repeat the same answer every time. "And I intended to practise what they teach," she added matter-of-factly. "I knowingly broke the Law of Communication and no doubt I would have broken the other Divinity Laws if you had not caught me. I am a deviant. I don't deny it. If you didn't already know that I wouldn't be here."

Hants sat back with a small smile. "Let's talk about Mr Summers then - your history teacher."

"You think he turned me."

"Didn't he?"

"No. He didn't."

"Then who did?"

"No one."

Hants involuntarily sat forward a little. "No one?" he repeated with forced amusement. This was not the answer he had been expecting. "Let me be more specific: Who introduced you to the concept of the divine? Who or what initiated your deviancy?"

Clara read past his sceptical amusement and saw a moment of uneasiness in those cool green eyes. She gave him a curious look which made him sit back again, as if distance might cover up his brief slip.

"Curiosity," she replied carefully. "I just wanted to know if it was true."

"If what was true?" Hants persisted. "What was the belief you were testing?"

"The Divinity Laws – their premise anyway," Clara replied, aware of the irony of her answer, and watching its effect on the agent. "I wanted to know if it was true that there's nothing sacred or divine out there. Haven't you ever wondered?"

Hants said nothing, but it did not matter, because as she spoke, Clara saw he understood her exactly.

"Every other year," she continued, "We get taught the Divinity Laws – what they're for, why they're important. And I just wanted to know if there really was nothing out there worth believing in. Was there nothing worth breaking the Laws for? So I asked."

Hants raised a cynical eyebrow, but his sneer did not fool Clara. She did not understand why, but she could read in his face that he already knew her answer. She was surprised: it was almost as if he not only understood what she was saying, but also knew it to be true. It did not make sense. He was a Divinity Agent. If he understood her, but without sympathy - if he knew the truth but denied it - what did that make him?

"Who did you ask?"

"I don't know...," she replied slowly. "The universe - the great nothing – whoever, whatever. I just asked."

"And you found an answer?"

"I got an answer," she said quietly.

"What was it?"

"A voice." She smiled at the mocking look that spread across his face, because she also saw the anxious flicker in his eyes. "Not in my head," she clarified. "As clear and audible as if you leant over and spoke in my ear now."

"And it said what?"

Clara tilted her head to one side a little and regarded Hants carefully, as if she were not sure she should answer his question.

"What did this 'voice' say?" Hants asked again, his voice a little steely.

"Clara," she replied simply. "It said my name."

Hants looked at her thoughtfully and gave a small smile of satisfaction. This was a real deviant. This wasn't just a phase, or teenage rebellion, or a passing fancy – this was a committed deviancy. She genuinely believed in her divinity, as if it were as real as the tangible world around her. And although her answer to his question bothered him, at least he could be triumphant that he had apprehended a genuine threat. She would get to know the inside of a rehabilitation camp particularly well. This sort took a long time to break, and, with the information Hants could now provide, her rehabilitation programme would be a rigorous one.

Hants had just one last question: "Where did Summers come in then?"

"It was an accident," Clara replied. "He dropped a book, I picked it up and some papers fell out." She nodded at the plastic wallets spread on the desk. "They were copies of a text and I realised we knew the same thing. We had a short exchange, established a collection point and that was it. We didn't speak again. He left things at the collection point and I collected them." She glanced down at her lap for a moment and then met his gaze one last time. "Can I see my parents now?"

*

They stood, the three of them in a huddle, just holding each other for what seemed an age; and Clara wished she could disappear into the arms around her and never leave their security. Eventually though, they broke apart, her mother keeping her hand grasped firmly in hers and her father pressing a steady hand to her back.

"Oh Clara, what happened to you?" her mother asked gently, instinctively brushing a strand of her daughter's short hair away from her face.

"I took up skateboarding," Clara said, feeling as though she was talking about something that happened years ago. "I made some friends ...and enemies...," she added, with a wry smile as she touched her face. "I cut my hair to hide from the police and I'm a deviant. And I'm sorry I didn't tell you..."

Her mother hugged her briefly again. "Sweetheart, we're sorry we weren't here. This would never have happened if we'd been here."

"Why didn't you tell us?" her father added.

"I didn't want you to cancel your trip - I thought I could wait. It's not your fault - it's been my decisions that got me here."

"I never thought this would happen," her mother mused sadly. "If only we'd known..."

"It's okay," her father interrupted calmly. "Everything's going to be okay." He looked intently at Clara. "You're a good girl, Clara. And you're strong - you can survive anything."

A policewoman opened the door. "One

more minute," she said gently, and closed the door again.

"Will you say goodbye to Greg for me?" Clara asked, forcing down the lump in her throat.

Her mother grabbed her and Clara clung to her desperately, suddenly realising this was it - for who knew how long.

"I'm sorry," she choked.

"Don't be," her mother said firmly. She pulled back and looked Clara in the eye. "We're only sorry we didn't know about it first..." She pursed her lips, as if to stop any words that might tumble out unchecked.

Her father stepped forward and wrapped his long arms around her. "It's going to be all right, Clara." He dropped his voice to a whisper: "Remember – they can't hurt you. You'll get through in one piece – you will."

He released her as the door opened again and the policewoman cleared her throat. Clara looked at her parents for the last time and a rush of questions flooded her mind that she didn't have time to ask.

Her mother mouthed 'I love you' as they paused at the door, and her father gave her a meaningful nod. Then the door shut behind them, and the click of its closing echoed through her whole body.

She was alone now and this was the start of her new life. From now on she would be known only as a deviant. Walls and locked doors were her new world and she would have to face it alone. There would be no family, no Carver, no Flinn to help her face it.

She touched the leather band on her wrist. They would be waiting though, waiting for her to get out. If she got out. Clara clenched her fist tightly to avoid her nervous tic starting up. She was ready for it: three months, six months, years, it didn't matter. Because the fact was, as Carver said, you couldn't kill the eternal, and she had the eternal on her side.

Epilogue

"...a week after being arrested by local police, the deviant teenager was sentenced today to three months in a juvenile rehabilitation camp..."

Flinn flicked off the screen and looked down at the deck of cards scattered at his feet, and then at the creased paper in his hand. He turned the paper over to show the map on the back and then flipped it back to the hand-scrawled letter, written in a neat, thoughtful hand. Flinn smiled and, sitting on the edge of his bed, ran his eyes over it again. It was not long, but that did not matter; it was something more than thirty seconds in the dark of an abandoned building. It was just enough to ease the passing of three months.

'Flinn,' it began.

'I don't know if this is going to be my only chance to say three things: I'm sorry, thank you and goodbye.

I'm sorry I didn't trust you enough to tell you everything. I didn't mean to deceive you – I just wanted to stay with you a little longer.

Thank you for teaching me the ollie, the board slide and most importantly – how to ride a halfpipe without falling off. I'm glad I got on that board the first time – even if it hurt. I'm glad you caught me where I shouldn't have been. But thank you, the most, for letting me be more than just a nice village girl – and for being my friend.

I know you might not understand what I am and why. I wish I could explain. Just remember this – someone once gave me some really good advice – to not overthink things and to just go with the feeling.

I don't know if this is a final goodbye or a 'see you later'.

I hope I'll see you later.

Same time, same place, perhaps.'

***Deviants**: The Divinity Laws #2*

Clara Slade is at the start of a three month prison sentence for breaking the Divinity Laws.

That's three months of *'rehabilitation'* - designed to *break* her.
Three months of *homesickness.*
Three months of *surviving day by day*, keeping her head down and staying out of trouble...

...except that - like a magnet - she seems to attract trouble: *hostile inmates, unhelpful rumours and dangerous secrets...*

And then there's the *Blackmoor Rehabilitation for Offenders Centre*; and the *'snap-back'*; and passing the *Exit Test...*

Just to keep her promise.
Just to get *home.*

If she can....

Looking for more stories, information, or got a question? Visit my blog:
pjkingblog.wordpress.com

18857247R00193

Printed in Poland
by Amazon Fulfillment
Poland Sp. z o.o., Wrocław